'Where's my s[on?]' her voice crac[ked]

'He's quite safe, Katrina.'

She recognised the voice that had answered, of course. How could she not?

She turned slowly towards the sound, steeling herself against the pain she would undoubtedly feel, but it wasn't just pain she felt when she saw Morgan standing in the doorway, holding Tomàs in his arms.

This hadn't been the way she had planned it would happen! She had wanted to broach the subject gently to Morgan, convince him that what she was about to ask him to do would be right before she let him meet the little boy. It was the only way that it might—just might—have worked.

'Your son is quite safe, Katrina,' he repeated when she didn't say anything.

Katrina shivered when she heard the harsh edge his voice held.

'Now, would you mind telling me what is going on? I think I have a right to know, don't you?'

Jennifer Taylor has been writing Mills & Boon®
romances for some time, but only recently 'discovered'
Medical Romance™. She was so captivated by these
heart-warming stories that she immediately set out to
write them herself! Having worked in scientific
research, Jennifer enjoys the research involved with the
writing of each book as well as the chance it gives her
to create a cast of wonderful new characters. When she
is not writing or doing research for her latest book,
Jennifer's hobbies include reading, travel and walking
her dog. She lives in the north west of England with
her husband.

Jennifer Taylor's website can be visited at:
www.jennifer-taylor.com

Recent titles by the same author:

THE BABY ISSUE
ADAM'S DAUGHTER
AN ANGEL IN HIS ARMS
THE ITALIAN DOCTOR

MORGAN'S SON

BY
JENNIFER TAYLOR

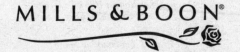

First published in Great Britain 2002
Harlequin Mills & Boon Limited,
Eton House, 18-24 Paradise Road, Richmond, Surrey TW9 1SR

© Jennifer Taylor 2002

ISBN 0 263 82717 8

Set in Times Roman 10½ on 11¼ pt.
03-0202-57546

Printed and bound in Spain
by Litografia Rosés, S.A., Barcelona

CHAPTER ONE

IT HAD been a long night.

Morgan Grey stepped under the shower and let the hot water pound his aching body. As head of orthopaedic surgery at Dalverston General Hospital he was used to working long hours, but that night had been exceptionally hard.

He had been called into work just after midnight to deal with the aftermath of a multiple pile-up on the motorway. Seventeen people had been injured in total, and most of them had suffered severe fractures, along with a range of other injuries. The theatres had seemed like conveyor belts as new patients were brought in, dealt with, then sent down to Recovery. In all honesty, Morgan couldn't recall half of the cases he had dealt with and that worried him. A lot. Patients were people, not just a set of broken bones that needed mending.

He sighed as he turned off the shower and reached for a towel. Maybe things would look better after a few hours' sleep, but right now he was both physically and mentally exhausted. He'd been running on adrenaline for most of the night and he knew enough about the dangers of continuing like that. Something was going to have to give soon.

He briskly towelled himself dry, thinking how pale his skin looked when he caught a glimpse of himself in the steamy mirror. It had been four years since he'd last had a holiday, and he'd not taken a real break since then. It had been his decision, of course, and he knew why he had made it. He'd needed to keep working so that he wouldn't have time to think about Katrina.

Morgan's mouth compressed as he wrapped the towel around his hips. The reflection in the mirror stared back at him and he didn't like what he saw. He had done the right thing about Katrina, the *only* thing, but the memory still hurt. He didn't need to glimpse the pain in his green eyes to prove that. Letting Katrina go had hurt more than anything would hurt him ever again, but he had done the right thing. He had!

He swore as he went to his locker and wrenched open the door. He must be more tired than he'd thought if he was standing there arguing with himself. What he needed was to go home and catch up on some sleep. Katrina was no longer a part of his life and he was no longer a part of hers. He had to accept that... He *had* accepted it!

He dressed quickly, not needing to think about what he was doing as he slid on his clothes. He had a wardrobe full of identical outfits back at his flat—rows of dark suits, racks full of plain white shirts and sober ties. It took the stress out of choosing what to wear each day and left him time for the important things, like work, for instance, although Katrina had teased him unmercifully about it...

Morgan slammed the locker shut and strode to the door, furious that his mind was running away with him again. He had just reached for the handle when the door opened and Robin White, his junior houseman, appeared.

'Sorry, sir, but A and E have been on the phone. They've had a woman and a child rushed in by ambulance. Another RTA, I'm afraid. The X-rays show that she's got a displaced fracture of the femur and they're concerned that there might be some femoral nerve damage. They want you to take a look at her.'

Morgan curbed his impatience with considerable effort. 'Where's Dr Fabrizzi? Can't he attend? I was just on my way home.'

'He's tied up in Theatre,' Robin explained apologetically. 'Complications with a patient he operated on earlier. I don't know how long he'll be but I can find out.'

'It doesn't matter,' Morgan snapped. He left the locker

room and strode along the corridor to the lift. He pressed the button then glanced at Robin, who had followed him. 'Scrub up. You'll be assisting me.'

'Yes!' Robin punched the air in delight then coughed, his face turning a rather alarming shade of puce. 'I mean, I'd be happy to, sir.'

Morgan smiled thinly as the younger man hurried away. It was good to know that somebody was happy in his work, he thought cynically, then realised how that thought had jarred. His work had been one of the most important things in his life since he had qualified. It had been the *only* important thing in the past few years, in fact. However, he had never stopped to wonder if he was truly happy.

He got into the lift, refusing to think about it. It wasn't in his nature to indulge in soul-searching and he didn't intend to start now. When the lift reached the ground floor he headed straight for the accident and emergency unit.

'You wanted me to look at a patient,' he said curtly to Sean Fitzgerald, the senior registrar on duty that day.

'Yes. Thanks for coming down.' Sean handed the notes he'd been writing to one of the nurses before leading the way. Morgan saw the young woman glance at him although she didn't acknowledge him.

Maybe his reputation for being unapproachable had circulated throughout the hospital, he found himself thinking as he followed the registrar to the smaller of the two trauma rooms, then wondered why he found the idea so unsettling when it had never bothered him before what people thought.

'I know how busy it's been in surgery so I wouldn't have called you if I hadn't thought it necessary. The fracture is close to the neck of the femur and it's going to need some pretty delicate surgery to make sure she doesn't suffer hip problems in the future,' Sean explained as he pushed open the door. 'I thought you'd be the best person to sort it out.'

Morgan didn't acknowledge the compliment and knew

that the younger doctor hadn't expected him to. They were all specialists in their own fields, although he knew without a shred of vanity that there were few surgeons who could match his skills. 'Let's have a look at her. What's her name, by the way?'

'We've no idea.' Sean shrugged. 'The police are searching for something to identify her, but so far they've not had much luck. She was driving a rental car and they haven't been able to get in touch with anyone from the depot yet. The car is a write-off. She's lucky to be alive, in fact.'

'How about the child? I believe there was a child brought in with her?' Morgan followed him into the room, barely glancing at the figure lying hooked up to an array of machinery in the high hospital bed.

'That's right, a little boy. He looks to be about three years old but it's hard to tell,' Sean explained. 'It's a miracle that he wasn't injured but, apart from a few bruises, he's absolutely fine. Unfortunately, he hasn't been able to tell us anything because he doesn't appear to speak English. We haven't understood a word he's said apart from ''Mama'', of course. Poor kid has been crying for her ever since he was brought in.'

Sean didn't add anything as he went to the light box on the far wall. 'I'll put up the X-rays so that you can see what I mean about the fracture.'

'Fine,' Morgan agreed. 'I just want to take a look at her first.'

One of the nurses was bending over the woman, making sure that the tube that was feeding her oxygen was securely taped into place, so he could see only the lower half of her body as he approached the bed. She had been draped with a sterile, green sheet but it had been folded back so that he could see the damage to her left leg.

His eyes skimmed over the badly swollen thigh while he made a rapid assessment of what he could be dealing with.

If the break was close to the neck of the femur then there was a risk that the blood supply to that area might have been cut off, as well as there being possible nerve damage. If it continued for any length of time then there was a danger that avascular necrosis could set in. That would cause the top of the femur to crumble at a later stage and it was something he wanted to avoid.

He shifted impatiently, wishing that the nurse would hurry up and finish what she was doing. He didn't doubt that his colleagues in A and E had done all they could, but he was eager to examine the patient himself. There was something about the way the woman's hand lay on top of the sheet, her fingers half-curled as though she were reaching out to him for help. To a man not normally given to flights of fantasy it made a strangely disturbing impact on his mind.

'Sorry, sir. I'll get out of your way now.' The nurse gave him a quick smile then stepped aside.

Morgan felt as though someone had punched him in the stomach as he got his first look at the woman's face. He swallowed hard when he felt bile rise to his throat. He wanted to turn around and run from the room rather than deal with the situation that had confronted him, but he couldn't do that. He had to make sure that his mind wasn't playing tricks.

He took a deep breath then forced himself to take stock of the honey-brown hair that was spilling over the pillow, the blue-veined eyelids, the sensually full mouth—cruelly distorted now by the tube that was helping her to breathe. Bit by bit his brain logged what he was seeing but he still had difficulty believing it.

'Sir? Do you want to take a look at the X-rays?'

Morgan wasn't sure how long he had been standing there before Sean Fitzgerald's voice seeped into his consciousness. He glanced round uncertainly, feeling sick and disorientated, feeling things that he hadn't wanted to feel ever

again in the whole of his life. He saw the look that passed
between the registrar and the nurse and knew that he must
appear every bit as shocked as he felt, but he couldn't do
anything about it.

'Is something wrong?' Sean began, but Morgan didn't
give him the chance to finish.

'Contact Dr Fabrizzi and tell him that he's needed here
right away,' he rapped out. 'He's in Theatre so tell him that
I'm on my way there and that I shall take over from him.'

'But aren't you going to operate on the patient yourself,
Dr Grey?' Sean stepped in his path, obviously loath to let
him leave like that. 'I don't understand.'

Morgan experienced an overriding urge simply to push
the younger man out of his way but he managed to control
it. 'It's quite simple, Dr Fitzgerald. The patient is my wife.
In the circumstances, it would be better if Dr Fabrizzi operated on her. I have every confidence in his ability to do
the job.'

He elbowed his way out of the door and strode across
the waiting room. He looked neither to right nor left and
wouldn't have seen anything if he had. All he could see in
his mind's eye was Katrina, lying so still on that bed, her
eyes shut, that tube taped to her beautiful mouth...

Bile rose into his throat once more and he veered off
towards the men's washroom and promptly threw up. He
leant against the wall afterwards and closed his eyes, feeling weak and drained, as though the very life had been
spewed out of him. Maybe it was shock, maybe it was a
whole lot of other things as well, but he had never felt
worse than he did at that moment.

A child's cry suddenly floated into the washroom, a thin,
reedy wail of terror, and his eyes opened abruptly. He took
a deep breath but it felt as though no air was getting to his
lungs all of a sudden. The child was still crying—Morgan
could hear him even though the word he was saying
sounded foreign and unfamiliar. On and on he cried, re-

peating it over and over again, 'Mama, Mama', until
Morgan felt that his head would explode with the sound.

He felt his eyes burn with tears of pain and anger as he
stood there and listened. The child was crying for his
mother. He was crying for Katrina. He was crying for
Morgan's wife but he wasn't Morgan's child.

There wasn't any doubt about that!

'It's true. Honestly. He just turned to Sean and said in that
frosty tone he has that she was his wife and that, in the
circumstances, Luke would be operating on her. I mean,
nobody even knew that he was married...'

The voices faded as the two nurses passed by the washroom. Morgan finished sluicing his face with cold water
and used a paper towel from the dispenser to dry himself
off. He checked his watch and was surprised to discover
that no more than five minutes had passed since he had
entered the washroom. Still, it was long enough. He needed
to get to Theatre and trade places with his second in com-
mand.

He straightened his tie then left the washroom and made
for the lift. He knew that he was putting off the moment
when he would have to find out more about the child but
he couldn't face it right then. How old had Fitzgerald said
the boy was, about three? It had been four years since he'd
seen Katrina so it was possible that she'd had a child in
the interim, of course. *Anything* was possible, except that
the child might be his!

A searing pain burned his gut at the thought. Morgan's
mouth compressed into a grim line as he fought to control
it. With his austerely handsome features he looked even
more forbidding as he strode towards the lifts. Several people stepped warily out of his way but he never even noticed
them. He was too consumed with not making a fool of
himself, with doing what had to be done, with doing his
duty. There would be time to feel, to hurt, to grieve later.

'Morgan! Wait up there.'

He swung round when he heard a familiar voice hailing him. 'I thought you were in Theatre,' he rapped out as Luke Fabrizzi caught up with him.

'I was, but I got through faster than expected.' The young American surgeon shrugged but Morgan couldn't help noticing the appraising look Luke gave him. The news about what had happened had obviously spread through the hospital at a rate of knots, not that he cared. People could say what they liked and it wouldn't make a scrap of difference to him or this situation.

'I'm taking the new patient up to Theatre now,' Luke continued. 'I believe she's your wife so is there anything I need to know? Dave Carson is doing the anaesthetic and he'll want to check that she isn't allergic to anything.'

'Katrina isn't allergic to anything,' he replied flatly. 'She's twenty-nine years old and, as far as I know, hasn't had any major surgery in the past. I can't speak about the last four years but prior to that she was extremely healthy.'

Luke nodded. 'Fine. At least it's something to go on.' He half turned to leave, then paused. 'We'll take good care of her, sir.'

Morgan inclined his head although he didn't reply. What could he have said? His colleagues didn't need his exhortations to do a good job. *Every* patient they treated received the best care possible.

He swung round as he felt an icy fear grip him. Katrina would be fine and there was no need for him to worry...

Only he couldn't help it.

He made his way to the coffee-shop in the foyer and sat at a table in the corner, aware that it would take very little for him to make a spectacle of himself. He was scared stiff by the thought of what was happening upstairs in Theatre, by the thought of what could go wrong. The fact that their success rate was well above the national average was no consolation. He knew the risks involved in surgery and every single one of them seemed to be floating around inside his head. The thought that Katrina might end up crippled was more than he could bear. The thought that she might die was too much even to consider.

He wasn't sure how long he sat there, torturing himself. It was only when he became aware of a figure standing beside him that he looked up. He frowned when he saw Luke Fabrizzi.

'Why aren't you in Theatre?' he snapped. His heart turned over and he pushed back his chair. 'Katrina…?'

'Is fine.' Luke smiled reassuringly. 'She came through the op with flying colours and, though I say so myself, I did a great job on her. It will take a bit of time to heal but…' He held out his hands, palms upwards.

Morgan felt a wave of intense relief flood through him so that it was a moment before he could speak. 'Thank you,' he managed at last.

'Hey, that's what we're here for!' Luke replied lightly. 'Anyway, she'll be going down to the IC unit in about an hour's time. OK?'

'Yes. And thanks again, Luke.'

He took a deep breath as he watched his colleague striding across the coffee-shop. Katrina was going to be fine. Now it was time to find out more about her son.

'He's in here, Dr Morgan. Amy is looking after him. He's fine, apart from some minor cuts and bruises and the fact that he's missing his mother.'

The same A and E nurse who had been at Katrina's bedside had shown him to the relatives' room. Morgan could see the curiosity in her eyes as she opened the door. It was obvious that she was intrigued by the situation but he couldn't have explained it even if he'd wanted to. He didn't know any more about what was going on than she did!

The child was sitting on the floor, sobbing listlessly. Morgan just had a second to absorb the damp black curls that clung to his head, the golden brown skin and chubby little body before the receptionist, who had been drafted in to look after him, looked up. He could tell at once that she'd heard what had happened and was making a conscious effort to act naturally.

'Has anyone found out his name yet?' he asked politely.

'I'm afraid not. The police have recovered a suitcase from the car but there were only some clothes and a few toys in it. They've promised to drop it off later.' The woman got awkwardly to her feet, blushing when he offered her his hand. 'Thank you, Dr Morgan. I...I'd better get back to work, then.'

She scurried out of the room, leaving him alone with the little boy. Morgan took a deep breath then went over to the child and crouched down beside him. 'It looks like it's just you and me now, doesn't it? I wonder what you can tell me about all this, eh?'

The little boy looked up at the sound of a strange voice and his face suddenly broke into a huge smile. Launching himself forward, he wrapped his chubby arms around Morgan's neck.

Morgan reacted instinctively, cradling the child to him as he rose to his feet. It had been years since he had held a child, not since he'd done a stint in paediatrics during his training, in fact, but it was surprising how it all came flooding back. It didn't seem strange to balance the sturdy little body on his forearm. It didn't even seem odd when he caught sight of them both in the mirror on the far wall. It was as though a dream he'd had a long, long time ago had suddenly come true.

'Papa.'

He blinked then stared at the little boy in shock. 'What did you say?'

'Papa!' On cue the child repeated the word, giggling delightedly as he buried his head in Morgan's shoulder.

Morgan took a deep breath, let it out slowly, then did

everything all over again. It didn't help. What the hell was going on? Why had this child—Katrina's son—called him Papa? Someone had a lot of explaining to do and it certainly wasn't him!

Katrina tried to swallow but her throat hurt too much, probably because of the tube that they had put down it. She knew that patients often had difficulty swallowing after they'd been intubated.

She frowned because that didn't make sense. She wasn't a patient. She was a nurse. She was the one who put in tubes and took them out.

She tried to sit up then groaned when she felt a searing pain shoot through her left leg. It felt strange, too, sort of rigid and heavy. Using the tips of her fingers, she tried to rub some life back into it but all she encountered was rough plaster of Paris rather than smooth flesh.

Her eyes flew open and she stared around, taking stock of all the machinery and tubes, the drip stand with its half-full bag of fluid. The line from it snaked downwards and she followed it like the games of snakes and ladders she had played as a child, then got another shock when she realised that it was disappearing into her vein.

Was she ill? Was that why she felt so peculiar?

'Ah, back in the land of the living, are you? Good.'

She frowned as a face suddenly came into view. 'Who are you?'

'That's different. Most people start with "Where am I?" Obviously, you're more the social type.' The man grinned at her. 'I'm Lee Anderson, the one and only male nurse on IC. But do not fear. I may be a mere man but I have a real Florence Nightingale touch when it comes to my patients.'

Katrina tried to smile. 'I'll believe you. So how did I get here?'

'You don't remember?' Lee was adjusting the drip while

he spoke but he paused to look at her. She sighed when she saw the sudden sharpening of his gaze.

'My name is Katrina Grey and I'm twenty-nine years old. I have one sister and two brothers, and I don't have amnesia. I'm just having a little trouble recalling what happened, that's all.'

'Mmm, sounds to me as though you know the score, Katrina Grey. You wouldn't happen to be a nurse, would you?' Lee grinned when she nodded. 'Thought so. I can spot one a mile off!'

His tone became briskly professional all of a sudden. 'OK, I'll give you a starter for ten, but don't tell anyone because it's strictly against the rules to jog a patient's memory. You were in a car crash. It appears that you and a lorry had a little contretemps and you came off worst. Ring any bells?'

'I'm not sure,' she began hesitantly, then gasped. 'Yes! I remember now. I was turning into the supermarket when this lorry ran into the back of me...' She felt a wave of sickness wash over her. 'Tomàs! Where is he? Where's my son?' she demanded, her voice cracking with fear.

'He's quite safe, Katrina.'

She recognised the voice that had answered, of course. How could she not? Hadn't she heard it in her dreams every single night for the past four years?

She turned slowly towards the sound, steeling herself against the pain she would undoubtedly feel, but it wasn't just pain she felt when she saw Morgan standing in the doorway, holding Tomàs in his arms. It was fear—pure, undiluted fear.

This hadn't been the way she had planned it would happen! she thought sickly. She had wanted to broach the subject gently to Morgan, explain the circumstances, convince him that what she was about to ask him to do would be right, before she let him meet the little boy. It was the only way that it might—just might—have worked. Now all that had gone by the board and she wasn't sure what to do.

'Your son is quite safe, Katrina,' he repeated when she didn't say anything. However, there was less reassurance in his voice than there might have been. Katrina shivered when she heard the harsh edge it held. It took an almost superhuman effort to disguise how scared she felt when he continued.

'Now, would you mind telling me what is going on? I think I have a right to know, don't you?'

CHAPTER TWO

'I...I...'

Katrina struggled to reply but the words seemed to be lodged deep in her throat. Panic was coursing through her and that combined with the shock of the accident and the after-effects of the surgery was a devastating combination. She heard Lee Anderson's exclamation of concern as her heart rate increased, causing the monitor to which she was attached to beep ominously.

'I'm sorry, sir, but I shall have to ask you to leave,' Lee said firmly, quickly resetting the machine. He looked up as one of the other IC nurses came hurrying over and shook his head to let her know that he had the situation under control.

Katrina saw the young woman look curiously from her to Morgan and had to bite her lip to hold back the hysterical laughter that suddenly threatened to overwhelm her. It was obvious that this situation had aroused a great deal of interest amongst the staff in the hospital and she couldn't help thinking how much Morgan must hate that. He had always been such a private person, building an invisible wall between himself and other people. Katrina had been the only one who had ever breached his defences, the only one he had opened up to.

A searing pain burned her heart at the thought. It took her all her time to summon a smile as he brought Tomàs to the bed so that she could kiss him. 'Be a good boy, *querido*,' she whispered as the child clung to her for a moment. '*Yo te amo*—I love you.'

She closed her eyes as Morgan settled the little boy back into his arms and curtly informed the male nurse that he

18

would return later. It seemed easier than having to face up to the fact that the problems wouldn't have gone away by the time he came back. Suddenly, she wasn't sure if she had enough strength to convince him to help her.

'He's gone now. The coast's clear.' Lee's tone was deliberately light but she heard the curiosity it held. She sighed as she opened her eyes and found Lee leaning against the wall by the bed, watching her.

'Was it that obvious that I didn't want to have to speak to him right now?'

'Yep.' Lee's face broke into an impish grin. He was a good-looking young man in his twenties with close-cropped fair hair that stood up in a spiky halo around his head. 'Even the machinery got the message. I haven't seen a heart rate increase like that without there being something *seriously* wrong with the patient. You must have broken an all-time record just now!'

Katrina managed a wobbly smile but her insides were still churning. 'Nice to know that I'll go down in the record books for something.'

'Oh, I reckon that you should score a double entry.' Lee shot an assessing glance at the machines before continuing once he was satisfied that everything was as it should be. 'You're the first person I've met who has managed to get a reaction out of Dr Grey. He's one cool customer normally.'

She wasn't sure what to say. She understood what Lee meant, of course, because Morgan *was* cool to the outside world. Her heart gave another sickening jolt. He had been far from cool with her, though.

Her mind swam as pictures she had held at bay these past four years rushed back to assail her. Her attraction for Morgan and his for her had been instantaneous. The minute they had met it had felt as though a light had gone on, and it had stayed like that throughout the whole time they were together. Even when they'd been at their lowest ebb they had still found passion in each other's arms. It had been a consolation but it hadn't been enough to keep their marriage alive.

Tears welled in her eyes and she turned her head so that Lee couldn't see them. It was pointless thinking like that, stupid to look back when she had to look forward. It wasn't her or Morgan who were important now but Tomàs. It was *his* future at stake, *his* life that would be for ever affected by the outcome of all this. She had to focus on that.

'Dr Khan will be along shortly to see you. He's head of the IC unit and he'll want to check you over.' Lee checked the drip again, giving her a moment to collect herself. 'If he's happy with your progress then I expect he will have you moved down to the surgical ward later today.' He smiled at her. 'We shunt our patients out of here as soon as we can, I'm afraid. You don't get to enjoy five-star luxury like this for a moment longer than is strictly necessary.'

Katrina summoned a smile, appreciating his tactfulness. 'So I've had my couple of hours of TLC, have I?'

'A couple of hours?' Lee's blond brows rose. 'You've been in the IC unit for two days, I'll have you know.' He sighed when she gasped. 'That's the problem with this place. Patients *never* appreciate just how much time and effort we spend on them because usually they're out for the count while they're here. What it must be like to work on a real ward and be suitably appreciated!'

She found it impossible to respond. She'd been in the IC unit for two whole days? If that was right then what had been happening to Tomàs during that time? Who had been taking care of him?

She didn't hear what Lee said after that and was barely aware of him moving away from the bed. She took a deep breath. Had Morgan been looking after the little boy for the past two days?

Her brain said no, that the idea was ridiculous, that it wasn't the sort of thing that he would have done, especially

in the circumstances. However, her heart said something
entirely different.

Katrina stared at the ceiling and let herself remember
how Morgan had looked as he'd stood there, holding
Tomàs in his arms. He had been angry, of course, but he'd
had a right to be. This must have been a shock for him
after all. But if she'd had to choose just one word to sum
up how he had looked then it would have to be 'natural'.
He had looked perfectly at ease and completely *natural*
holding the little boy.

And the tears that she had held in check just moments
before spilled over and rolled down her cheeks.

Morgan paced his office, unable to relax. There was no
point reminding himself that Sanjit Khan was a very busy
man and would phone when he got the chance—he needed
to know the prognosis. Luke Fabrizzi had assured him that
the operation on Katrina's femur had gone extremely well
and Morgan didn't doubt him. However, restoring a patient
to full health required more than simply putting bones, tendons and nerves back together. It required teamwork, dedicated teamwork at that, and Khan was a vital link in the
process.

'Papa?'

He stopped pacing as a small hand tugged at his trouser
leg. Bending down, he summoned a smile, praying that the
little boy couldn't tell how much it tore at his heart each
time he addressed Morgan that way. He had no idea why
Tomàs believed that he was his father, but he simply
couldn't find it in his heart to correct the child and possibly
upset him.

Maybe he didn't *want* to correct him, a small voice whispered in his head. Maybe he wanted the mistake to continue
indefinitely. Hadn't it been his dearest wish that one day
he and Katrina would have a child?

The thought was so painful that he had to make a conscious effort to disguise his feelings for the child's sake. Damn Katrina! he thought viciously as he admired the picture which the little boy had drawn. If she had deliberately set out to hurt him, she had certainly achieved her objective!

'Very pretty, Tomàs—*muy bonita. Si?*' He dredged up a few words of school Spanish, smiling when the little boy laughed joyously. The child had a wonderfully sunny nature and giggled at the simplest things. He particularly enjoyed Morgan's pitiful attempts to talk to him, chuckling away as the man stumbled through a mismatched assortment of verbs and tenses.

Still, they'd managed together over the last few days, and managed surprisingly well, all things considered. As the telephone rang and he stood up to answer it, he found himself thinking how amazing it was that he and this child had formed a bond in such a short space of time.

'Morgan Grey,' he announced crisply, feeling his heart racing when he realised that it was Sanjit Khan on the line at last. He listened intently to what the other man had to say, feeling some of his tension dissipate when he realised that the prognosis was far better than he had dared hope.

During the two days that Katrina had been unconscious he had run through a host of possible complications. That was the trouble with knowing so much about what could go wrong with the human body—it gave one's mind the licence to home in on the very worst scenarios. However, it appeared that his fears had been premature and that she was well on the way to making a full recovery.

He thanked Sanjit and hung up, aware that his hands were shaking. It shocked him that he should be reacting like that because it was so out of character. He was *always* in control, always able to subdue his own feelings and focus on what needed to be done, but not when it concerned Katrina. She had been the one person who could make him lose control.

He swore softly as he scooped up the child. Opening his office door, he paused briefly by his secretary's desk, ignoring the curiosity in her eyes. He knew that the whole hospital was buzzing with gossip about what had happened but there was little he could do about it.

'I shall be at home for the rest of the day, Mrs Adams. Dr Fabrizzi has kindly agreed to cover for me so, please, refer any calls to him.'

'Certainly, sir.' Trisha Adams had been a model secretary during the three years she had worked for him. However, curiosity got the better of her that day. 'How is your wife, Dr Grey?'

'A lot better, thank you.' Morgan smiled coolly at the woman, noting but not responding to her disappointment when he didn't say anything more. A wry smile twisted his mouth as he left the office. The truth was that he *still* didn't know what was going on so he couldn't have told her anything even if he had wanted to!

He made straight for the lifts, pausing when Luke and Robin White suddenly appeared from the direction of Theatres. They both stopped when they saw him and Luke smiled at the little boy.

'Holà, pequeño! Como estàs?'

Morgan's brows rose steeply. 'I didn't know you spoke Spanish.'

'Only enough to get by, I'm afraid. I did a stint at a hospital in Miami during my days as an intern and picked up the odd phrase,' Luke explained. He waited until Robin had excused himself and hurried away before continuing, 'Sanjit just told me the good news about your wife. It must have been a relief.'

'It was. I know that you did a damn fine job...'

'But there's still a lot that could have gone wrong,' Luke finished soberly. He glanced at the little boy and sighed. 'Tell me to mind my own business, but I get the impression this has come like a bolt out of the blue?'

'It has.'

It wasn't in his nature to discuss his private life but suddenly Morgan found that he needed to tell someone. Maybe it would help him understand what was going on if he used Luke as a sounding board. He was on the verge of pouring it all out when Luke's beeper sounded.

'A and E,' the younger man announced, checking its display. 'I'll have to go but I could call round to your place tonight, if you'd like me to. Maggie has a fitting for her wedding dress after work and heaven knows how long that will take!'

Morgan felt a stab of envy when he heard the warmth in the other man's voice as he spoke about his fiancée. He couldn't help wondering if he had spoken about Katrina that way once upon a time.

He drove the thought from his mind, knowing how much damage it could do. He had to find a balance in all this and if talking to Luke would help then it would be worth forfeiting his cherished privacy.

'I would appreciate that. Around seven, shall we say?' He smiled when Luke nodded. 'I want to pop back here later to see Katrina, and then there's the herculean task of persuading this young man that he should go to bed. If there's a knack to it, I certainly haven't discovered it as yet!'

'It's early days!' Luke laughed. 'What you need is a bit more practice. Catch you later, then.'

He loped off down the stairs, leaving Morgan to follow at a more leisurely pace. He stepped into the lift, grabbing hold of Tomàs's hands to keep them away from the doors as they closed. The child chattered away to him in rapid Spanish, obviously excited about something, but although he tried his best, he couldn't understand half of what the little boy was saying to him.

He sighed as the lift reached the ground floor and they stepped out into the busy foyer. Maybe practice would help

him deal with the practical aspects of what had happened
but he still had no idea what was going on. Katrina was
the one who held the key to all this, the only person who
could explain. Whilst a part of him could barely contain
his impatience to hear what she had to say, another part
was afraid.

Katrina had brought to his life the greatest joy and the
deepest pain. He had every right to fear what she would
tell him.

'There. That's better, isn't it? Just let me pack a couple of
pillows behind you then you'll be able to sit up and see
what's happening in the big wide world.'

'Thanks.' Katrina smiled weakly as the nurse deftly slid
some pillows behind her back. The transfer from the IC
unit had been as smooth and stress-free as possible, but she
had to admit that she felt as though she had done a hard
day's work. She couldn't recall feeling so exhausted before
and it worried her.

'I feel so washed out,' she admitted as the nurse tucked
in the sheets. 'I don't seem to have any energy left.'

'And you think that's strange?' The nurse gave a throaty
laugh. She was a comfortably plump, black woman in her
thirties with a wonderful smile. The badge pinned to the
pocket of her pale blue uniform blouse said that her name
was Beatrice Bosanko. 'You've had major surgery, my girl,
so it isn't surprising that you feel as weak as a kitten!'

'I suppose so. It's just that I'm not used to feeling like
this.' She grimaced. 'I'm normally very healthy, you see.'

'*Normally* you don't go ten rounds with an articulated
lorry,' Beatrice replied drily, making her laugh. 'That's better. We can't have our patients looking down in the dumps.
It's bad for our reputation and Dr Grey certainly wouldn't
approve of that!'

Beatrice stopped when she realised what she had said.
Katrina summoned a smile, not wanting her to feel embar-

rassed. 'Morgan does have a way of making his feelings clear.'

'Um, yes he does.' Beatrice gave the bedclothes a final twitch then hurried away. Katrina saw her stop and say something to the other nurse on duty, saw them both turn to glance her way, and sighed. It looked as though this situation was going to be difficult for everyone, not just for her and Morgan.

As though thinking about him had somehow conjured him up, he suddenly appeared. She felt her heart start to race as he stopped at the desk and had a word with the two nurses. She took a deep breath, using the vital few seconds' grace to get herself in hand, but it was hard to maintain her composure as she watched him walking down the ward towards her. It had been four years since she had seen him prior to that morning and now she found herself drinking in the changes those years had wrought with a greedy urgency.

He was as lean as ever, she quickly noted, maybe a little leaner, in fact. At six feet two he had the muscular build of an athlete, with wide shoulders and chest tapering down to a trim waist and hips. However, she couldn't help noticing that his dark suit seemed to hang a shade too loosely on him, as though he might have lost weight.

As usual he was impeccably groomed, his dark hair brushed smoothly back from his face, emphasising the high cheekbones and square jaw, the thin but perfectly sculpted mouth. It was only as he drew nearer that she could see the silver wings at his temples, the new lines that had been etched around his eyes, not to mention the faintly hollow expression they held. It was obvious to her that Morgan had suffered a great deal of unhappiness in the past four years and it was little consolation to know that it had been his stubbornness which had been the main cause of it.

'How are you feeling?' he asked curtly when he reached

her bed. He picked up the chart and skimmed through the notes that had been sent down with her from the IC unit then glanced at her.

'Weak and a bit wobbly, but I'll survive,' she replied as calmly as she could. Nevertheless, she couldn't stop her heart from skittering around inside her chest when he drew the curtains round the bed and sat down. It was obvious that he intended to find out what was going on and she knew that there was no way she could refuse to tell him. However, it was how he would react which scared her most. Knowing him as she did—his stubbornness, his obstinacy, his determination always to do the right thing—she had every reason to be worried!

'The child believes that I am his father. Why?'

He didn't try to lead up to the question, mainly, she suspected, because it had been eating away at him for the past few days. She could only try to imagine the pain he felt because he gave no sign of it as he sat there, his green eyes distant, his expression remote. Other people might believe that he was unfeeling but she had never made that mistake, not even when he had wanted her to believe it. Morgan felt and he felt deeply, and this was going to hurt him. Yet even though she knew that, she had no choice.

'Because he saw a photograph of you and asked who you were. I told him that you were my husband and he somehow got it into his head that you were his father.' She made no attempt to excuse her actions and heard his breath exhale in a sharp hiss which could have stemmed from surprise or displeasure.

'Why didn't you explain that he'd made a mistake? Was it some sort of a game, Katrina? Or a fantasy even, something you dreamed up so...' Morgan couldn't go on. Katrina guessed that he couldn't bring himself to finish the sentence and accuse her of what was in his mind now and what had been in hers for the past four years.

'So that I could pretend that you hadn't told me that you

no longer wanted me? Is that what you are finding it so difficult to say?' Her voice echoed with pain and she saw him wince. For a man who was always so controlled, it was hugely revealing.

'I never said that, Katrina. You know why I decided that our marriage must end.' His tone was clipped but she could imagine the anguish he was feeling at that moment.

'Yes. And it was unforgivable of me to have said that, Morgan. I'm sorry.' She touched his hand, feeling the iciness of his skin, the tautness of the sinews beneath it. Morgan was holding onto his control with a grim determination that was costing him an awful lot of effort, and she wasn't making it any easier by acting this way.

She withdrew her hand abruptly, feeling tears stinging her eyes. 'I'm sorry,' she repeated, because she couldn't think of anything else to say.

'Forget it. It doesn't matter. Just tell me what this is all about, Katrina.'

His tone was firm and for some reason it helped to steady her. She quickly marshalled her thoughts, knowing that it was crucial that she put her case to him as calmly as possible. Morgan had always been uncomfortable with emotion and had difficulty dealing with it, so she had decided from the outset that she would need to appeal to the logical side of his nature.

'It will be easier if I start at the beginning so bear with me while I backtrack a few years,' she said quietly. 'After we split up, I took a job with an aid agency that was working in South America with homeless children. Their aim was to provide medical care for the children and educate them so that they could have a better life.'

'I didn't know.'

She heard the shock in his voice and sighed. 'There was no point in telling you. Our marriage was over by then so what I did was no longer your concern.'

His hands clenched until she could see his knuckles

gleaming whitely through his skin. 'I did what was right, Katrina.'

'You did what you *thought* was right,' she corrected gently, although she was surprised by his response because she had expected him to react with his customary detachment.

'Anyway, that's not important now. It's easier if I stick to the facts.' She clamped down on a sudden feeling of unease, knowing that she couldn't afford to be sidetracked. She would get nowhere if she started worrying about why he wasn't reacting in a certain way.

'Whilst I was working over there I met a young girl called Rosa. She was barely into her teens but she had been living on the streets for several years by then. Most of the children we dealt with ended up living in shanty towns on the edge of landfill areas. They make a living—if you can call it that—by picking through the rubbish.'

She paused, feeling a wave of weakness wash over her all of a sudden. Morgan got up without a word and poured her a glass of water. His mouth compressed as he saw how her hand was shaking when she tried to take it from him.

'I'll hold it.' He held the glass to her lips, steadying her as she raised her head to sip from it.

Katrina felt a frisson race through her when she felt his long fingers curling around the back of her head. She could feel the separate imprint of each finger pressing against her skull and she almost cried out as her mind instantly recognised his touch. The feel of his hands was imprinted on her consciousness and she could never forget it, no matter what.

'Enough?' The rawness in his voice told its own tale and she nodded weakly as he put the glass back on the bedside locker. He sat down again, deliberately avoiding her eyes by focusing on a spot a little to her right. 'Go on.'

She took a deep breath but it was hard to think clearly as memories clamoured to the forefront of her mind. It wasn't right that she should remember in such exquisite, sensual detail how Morgan's hands had felt on her body when they had made love, but she couldn't help it!

'R-Rosa lived quite close to where we had our offices. She shared a hut made from bits of old plastic sheeting with her brother, Romano, who was a year older than her. She was a pretty little thing, or she would have been if she'd had enough to eat and someone to look after her.'

It helped to concentrate on the story so she carried on, hoping that it would ease the ache from her body. 'Unlike a lot of the children we saw, Rosa wanted to learn and was eager for me to show her things. That's why I spent more time with her than any of the other children and why I suppose that she came to trust me. Most of the children living there didn't trust adults, you see.'

'I can imagine.' He glanced at her then but his eyes were hooded so she had no idea what he was thinking 'What does Rosa have to do with this situation, with Tomàs?'

A smile curled her mouth as she heard how natural the name had sounded coming from his lips. She had a feeling that he had used it often in the past few days and that was a good sign, surely?

'Rosa was Tomàs's mother,' she explained simply, trying not to let herself get too hopeful at such an early stage.

'But I thought you said that she was just a teenager?' he demanded incredulously, then sighed. 'Does that sound as naïve as I imagine it does?'

'No. It's right to be shocked. It's only wrong if you accept the situation and don't try to do something about it,' she said swiftly.

'As you tried to do?' he said astutely.

She shrugged. 'One of our main aims was to provide those kids with sex education, but it wasn't easy to make them understand the risks. Most of the girls got pregnant in their teens and it was simply accepted that it would happen.

'It broke my heart when Rosa told me that she was having a baby, yet in a funny way it was a good thing it happened. She was fourteen years old when Tomàs was born, and from the day he came into the world she was determined that he was going to have a better life than she'd had.'

'You keep using the past tense so do I take it that the girl is dead?' he asked gently.

'Yes.' Her eyes filled with tears once more and this time she couldn't hold them back. 'Rosa died last year. She contracted meningitis and there was nothing we could do for her.'

'What a sad end to a young life,' he said, reaching over and taking hold of her hand.

Katrina stiffened but he didn't appear to have realised what he had done. It had been an instinctive gesture of comfort and the fact that he had felt able to show his feelings to this extent after everything that had happened gave her the courage to carry on.

'It was very sad. I think Rosa knew that she wasn't going to get better because she made me promise that if she died I would look after Tomàs.' She shrugged when he looked at her. 'I'd spent a lot of time with him and Rosa so I was like a second mother to him. He'd called me Mama from the time he'd started to talk.'

'And nobody objected to you taking care of him?' he put in.

'There was nobody to object. Rosa's brother didn't want the responsibility of looking after him, and as for their parents... Well, there had been no contact with them for years. Granted, the aid agency weren't very happy when they found out, but there was little they could do about it. Of course, I knew there might be problems taking Tomàs out of the country, so the local priest arranged for me to adopt him.'

'So he is legally your son? Is that what you are saying, Katrina?'

She heard the grating note in his voice and knew how he must be feeling, but she couldn't afford to worry about that now. 'So far as the authorities over there are concerned, yes. However, the Foreign Office isn't happy with the paperwork that I have. Basically, they're questioning the validity of it. They have granted me a temporary order allowing Tomàs to remain in the country for a period of six months.'

'So what do you intend to do?' Morgan frowned as he considered what she had told him.

'I've consulted a solicitor and it appears that the only way that I can keep him here permanently is by applying to the UK courts to adopt him. I'll need to have an assessment done and all sorts of other formalities but it's my best hope.'

She paused, wondering how best to phrase the next bit, but there was no easy way to set about it. 'My solicitor also advised me that the courts would look more favourably on my application if Tomàs were to be adopted by two parents, a mother and a father.'

'A mother and a father,' he repeated blankly. She saw the colour suddenly leach from his face. 'I understand now. You're telling me that you want a divorce, Katrina. Of course, I'll—'

'No! That wasn't what I meant at all.' She gripped onto his hand as he tried to withdraw it, uncaring that her nails were cutting half-moons into his skin.

'I don't want a divorce, Morgan! That's the last thing I want. I want you to help me adopt Tomàs. I want you to agree to be his father!'

CHAPTER THREE

'No!'

Morgan shot to his feet, uncaring that he almost upset the chair in the process. He stared at Katrina, wondering sickly if she had dreamed this up deliberately to hurt him and make him pay for the way he had hurt her. How could she have asked that of him after all they had been through?

'Morgan, please! I know this must have been a shock...'

'You're right about that!' His voice cracked like a whip and he saw her shrink back against the pillows. 'It just amazes me that you had the gall to suggest such a thing. Why did you do it, Katrina? Does it give you some sort of perverted pleasure to cause me pain?'

'No, of course not. I never wanted to hurt you, Morgan. I...I care too much about you.'

All the colour seemed to drain from her face so that her hazel eyes seemed inordinately bright all of a sudden. With a sickening return of sanity, he remembered how ill she had been.

He swore softly and succinctly yet his anger was directed at himself now rather than at her. How could he have forgotten that she had just come through major surgery, that a scene like this was the last thing she needed at this stage in her recovery?

'Just calm down,' he said firmly, lifting her hand from the bed so that he could check her pulse. His mouth compressed when he felt how it was racing. He was suddenly beset by a feeling of self-loathing the like of which he had never felt before. How *could* he have put his feelings before her safety?

'If I promise to calm down, will you try to do the same?'

Her voice was husky, the tears she was trying so hard to hold back coating each word. Morgan closed his eyes as he felt the pain knifing deep inside him once more. The one thing he had never wanted to do had been to hurt her and yet it was the one thing he had been unable to avoid.

'Yes. Now, try to relax.' He glanced round as the curtain was tentatively moved aside and Beatrice popped her head round the opening.

'Is everything all right, Dr Grey?' she asked, shooting a worried glance at Katrina.

'Fine, thank you.' He released Katrina's wrist and picked up the chart from the end of the bed, needing something tangible to focus on. His head was whirling with a conflict of emotions so that he was having difficulty thinking straight. 'Has Mrs Grey been written up for any sedatives?'

'Dr Fabrizzi is due at any moment so I expect he'll review the patient's medication then, sir,' Beatrice told him formally.

'I'll have a word with him when he arrives then. Thank you, Nurse,' he replied coolly, making it clear that it was meant as a dismissal.

He saw Beatrice shoot another worried glance at Katrina before she retreated, and struggled to hold back a bitter laugh. Was the nurse afraid that he was going to say something else to upset her patient? She needn't be. He'd said all he intended to for now, although he wasn't foolish enough to believe that it would be the end of the matter!

Pain lanced through him once again as he recalled what Katrina had said but he managed to disguise it as he turned to her. He was pleased to see that a little colour had come back to her face although she still looked alarmingly fragile, markedly so when he recalled how full of life she had been in the past. Katrina's *joie de vivre* had been one of the many things he had loved about her from the moment they had met.

It was an effort to hide how much the memory disturbed

him but he was a master at hiding his feelings. 'I want you to relax and try not to worry,' he repeated in the decisive tone he used when dealing with a particularly fractious patient. 'You have just undergone major surgery and it is going to take some time for your body to recover from the shock.'

'I know that. I *am* a nurse, Morgan, in case you've forgotten.'

There was a bite in her voice now that pleased him because he could tell that she was recovering her composure. 'I hadn't forgotten. However, it is an entirely different situation when you are cast in the role of a patient.' His tone was so bland that he couldn't understand why it should make her smile.

'Don't remind me! Remember that time you came down with flu?' Her laughter was like a burst of summer sunshine after a rain storm, instantly making his heart lift.

'And I was the world's worst patient?' he admitted ruefully.

'That's an understatement! You were an absolute fiend, Morgan, continually fretting about not being able to go to work and having to stay in bed...'

'Until you found the perfect solution to keep me there,' he cut in without thinking.

'Yes. Bed was the one place where we were able to forget the world and its problems, wasn't it, Morgan?'

Her tone was gentle, reflective. It might have been a simple statement of fact but he felt his body clench on a feeling of longing so intense that it was all he could do not to gasp.

His passion for Katrina—and hers for him—had been the colour in their lives, like a rainbow that they'd drawn down from the sky and wrapped around them. And the worst thing was that he knew with a sudden flash of insight that it would be the same now as it had been then. The passion wouldn't have died even if their hopes and dreams had.

He turned away, terrified of how vulnerable it made him
feel to acknowledge that fact. He couldn't afford to let anything cloud his judgement in this situation.

'Morgan, I won't give up. I know that I'm doing the
right thing. I only hope—*pray*—that you will realise that
before it's too late. It's Tomàs's whole future at stake here.'

He paused with his back to her, one hand gripping the
floral curtain as he fought for control. 'You're wasting your
time, Katrina. I'm sorry but I can't help you.'

'Just promise me that you'll think about it,' she urged.

'I don't need to.' He turned to look at her and his green
eyes were full of a pain so raw that he was unable to hide
it. 'It wouldn't be right.'

'Why not? Look, if you're worried that I expect you to
take responsibility for Tomàs then don't be. All I want from
you is your name, Morgan. I don't expect anything else.'
Her eyes met his and he saw the determination they held.
'I know how you feel about adoption but this is different.
Tomàs will be your son in name only. He won't have any
claim on you emotionally or financially!'

Morgan didn't reply. He couldn't. Words were beyond
him at that moment. He swished the curtain aside and
strode down the ward, forgetting that he had intended to
wait and have a word with Luke Fabrizzi until he had left
the building and was unlocking his car.

He slid behind the wheel, wondering if he should go
back yet terrified that he wouldn't be able to handle it if
he did. Could he really function as the objective professional when it felt as though his insides were being syste-
matically ripped to shreds?

He started the engine then glanced in the rear-view mirror before backing out of the parking space, feeling his
heart knot painfully when he saw a man and a child walking
past behind the car, hand in hand. He closed his eyes but
the image was imprinted on his retinas. Father and son. The

embodiment of his and Katrina's dreams. The one thing they had been destined to be denied.

He backed out of the space and headed down the drive. His eyes felt as though they were on fire, burning with tears he had never been able to shed, not then, not now. Tears were a sign of weakness and grown men didn't cry. How many times had he been told that as he'd been growing up? He had no idea. The one thing he did know was that they wouldn't help a jot in this situation.

He took a deep breath then made himself recite the facts, not that there was any danger that he had forgotten them.

He was sterile.

He couldn't father a child.

He could never give Katrina the family she wanted so desperately.

His hands clenched on the steering-wheel. It was no wonder that she had pinned her hopes on adopting Tomàs, and it broke his heart to know that once again he was going to have to disappoint her.

'How long do you think I'll need to stay in hospital?'

Katrina summoned a smile but it was an effort. Morgan had been gone only a few minutes before Luke Fabrizzi, the doctor in charge of her case, had arrived. She'd done her best to answer his questions about how she was feeling but she knew that she'd skated over the truth. She still felt sick and shaken by that confrontation with Morgan. She'd known from the outset that it wouldn't be easy to convince him to help her, but she'd never suspected that it would turn out as badly as it had.

She blinked back tears of frustration as Luke hung the clipboard back on the end of the bed then smiled at her. 'I wish I had a dollar for every time a patient has asked me that question. I'd be rich by now!'

'Sorry,' she apologised, and saw him shake his head.

'Hey, I was only teasing. Anyhow, I'd plan on spending

the next three weeks in here if I were you. As you know, the fracture was just below the neck of the femur,' Luke explained. 'It's been pinned and plated, and I was very pleased with how the operation went, but it's going to take time to heal. You're looking at four to five months before you'll be able to put any weight on it and even then you'll need to be extremely careful.'

'Four to five months!' she exclaimed, stricken. 'But what about work? I can't possibly take all that time off.'

'I'm afraid you don't have any choice.' Luke sounded sympathetic. 'I believe you're a nurse so you must know how important it is that the bone is allowed to heal fully. Trying to rush the process could lead to problems in the future, and that's the last thing we want to happen.'

He paused and she had a feeling that he was choosing his words with care. 'Morgan didn't mention where you were working at the moment but I'm sure they'll understand and make allowances. After all, nobody chooses to end up in a hospital bed.'

'I expect so,' she said sadly, aware that Morgan hadn't said anything because he'd had no idea. He knew nothing about the life she had led these past four years, just as she knew nothing about what had been happening to him during that time. It was hard to believe that once they had been so close that even a few hours spent apart had seemed like an eternity.

Still, that was the least of her problems, she decided, deliberately focusing on the present rather than the past. Life was going to be extremely difficult if she was unable to work for such a lengthy period. She had been hoping to find a job with a nursing agency once she had made suitable provision for Tomàs. It had seemed like the best option because at least she would be able to choose the hours she worked to fit in with caring for the little boy. Obviously, that was out of the question now and she had no idea how she was going to manage with no money coming in and very little in the bank to fall back on.

It was yet another worry to add to all the others that were crowding her head. Katrina tried to rest after Luke Fabrizzi left but her mind was racing with everything that had happened that day. If only there was a way to convince Morgan that he should help her then her biggest problem would have been solved, but she knew how stubborn he could be once he had made up his mind.

She sighed.

Stubborn really wasn't the word for the man!

Morgan still hadn't managed to persuade Tomàs that it was time for bed when Luke arrived that evening. He went to open the door with the little boy clinging grimly to his neck.

'Come in,' he invited, moving aside so that the other man could step inside the hall.

Luke grinned as he shut the door. 'I see he's still wide awake. What time does he normally go to bed?'

'Any time he chooses, basically,' Morgan replied ruefully, leading the way to the sitting room. He tried to put the little boy down on the floor, only to be met by a howl of protest. Scooping the child back into his arms, he looked at Luke in despair. 'He seems terrified that I'm going to leave him. Every time I've tried to put him down tonight, he starts crying.'

'Understandable, I guess. It must have been a shock for him to have been parted from his mother like that.'

'I suppose so.' Morgan sighed as he sat on the sofa and settled the little boy on his lap. He'd not had time to change since he'd got home and his once pristine shirt was creased to a rag thanks to the child's clutching hands. He could do with a shower, not to mention a drink, after the day he'd had but both were out of the question until he had got

Tomàs settled. Still, his needs came way down the list of priorities at the moment.

'I suppose I've been lucky because he's been very good up till now,' he said, smoothing the curls back from the child's forehead. 'But he's been very clingy ever since I got back from the hospital this afternoon for some reason. I'm not sure what's wrong with him, to be honest.'

'Maybe he sensed that you were upset,' Luke suggested. 'Kids are very perceptive and they soon pick up on things like that.'

Morgan grimaced. 'You could be right. I was a bit up-tight when I got in.' He glanced at the little boy and sighed. 'Mrs Mackenzie, my daily, was looking after him while I was out, and she said that he'd been fine with her.'

'It can't be easy, dealing with this situation.' Luke looked at him levelly. 'One of the nurses told me that you appeared rather upset earlier on and I could tell that Katrina was worried about something when I saw her.'

'I expect she was.' He stood up abruptly and walked to the window, the child clinging to him every step of the way. He took a deep breath but he felt as though he would burst if he didn't tell someone what had happened that day. 'She wants me to help her adopt Tomàs, and I told her that I couldn't do it.'

'Couldn't? Or wouldn't?' Luke asked quietly.

'Both. It's out of the question.' Morgan swung round, unable to conceal his impatience. 'Katrina knows my views on adoption!'

'So it's something you two have discussed before?' Luke queried.

'Yes.'

He turned to stare out of the window again, wondering if he was making a mistake by discussing something so personal with an outsider. But he needed help and he needed it fast because the situation was driving him crazy.

'I can't father a child, you see. I've had all the tests done and they've proved conclusively that I'm sterile.'

'It must have been a blow for you,' Luke observed sympathetically. 'I know it would be for me.'

'It was.' Morgan took a deep breath then carried the little boy back across the room and sat down again. Tomàs snuggled closer, burrowing his warm little body against him in a way that Morgan found oddly comforting. Maybe it was that which helped him speak about something he had never discussed with anyone apart from Katrina.

'I was devastated when I found out. I couldn't really believe it at first even though Katrina and I had been trying for a child for some time by then. It simply hadn't crossed my mind that there might be something wrong with me. I had all the tests redone but the results came back the same. Short of a miracle happening, there's no way that I can ever father a child.'

'Is that what caused you two to split up? Couldn't she handle the thought of not having a child of her own? A lot of women couldn't.'

He shook his head. 'No. Katrina was heartbroken, of course, but she was as much upset for me as for herself.'

He cleared his throat, embarrassed by the wealth of emotion he could hear in it. It was hard to talk about that black period in his life and detach himself from how he had felt at the time. 'She told me that it made no difference whatsoever to her feelings for me. However, I knew that it would be wrong to play on that fact.

'She had always longed for a family of her own, you see, so I decided that the only thing I could do in the circumstances was to end our marriage. It wasn't fair to keep her tied to me.'

Luke frowned. 'But you two are still married, aren't you? I thought you told the staff in A and E that she was your wife?'

He smiled thinly. 'I see the grapevine is as reliable as

ever. But you're quite right. I did tell them that, and it's true. My solicitor was unable to serve Katrina with the divorce papers because she'd disappeared. I now know that she'd left the country but at the time I had no idea where she'd gone.'

He paused as he recalled those dark months. He had wanted desperately to track her down but he had known that it would be the wrong thing to do. He'd had to make a clean break, give Katrina her freedom, not keep her tied to him. He realised that Luke was waiting for him to continue and shrugged.

'I left it at that and didn't pursue the matter. Legally, at least, we are still man and wife.'

'And now she wants your help to adopt this little fellow?' Luke said softly, glancing at the little boy. The child's eyelids were drooping but he still had a tight hold of Morgan's neck.

'That's right.' Morgan quickly explained what Katrina had told him that afternoon, doing his best to keep his account as impartial as possible. It wasn't easy but if Luke offered him any advice then he wanted it to be unbiased by anything he had said. He saw the younger man frown when he came to the end of the tale, and tensed in anticipation.

'Why are you so opposed to the idea?' Luke shrugged when he looked at him. 'Katrina has said that she doesn't intend to involve you either financially or emotionally, and I'm sure that you can trust her to keep her word. Basically, she just needs your help to safeguard the child's future, so I can't really see what is the problem.'

'Because it would be wrong!' Morgan's tone was sharp. He couldn't help wondering if Luke was being deliberately obtuse. 'I would be telling a lie because I wouldn't be his father. All I would be to Tomàs is a name on a piece of paper!'

'And that's what is worrying you most, is it?' Luke guessed.

'Wouldn't it worry you?' he countered, avoiding a direct answer because he couldn't bring himself to explain why the idea was so abhorrent. He had never spoken about his childhood to anyone. Even Katrina didn't know the full story and he'd told her more than he'd told any other human being.

He frowned when it struck him that maybe he'd brought all this on himself by holding back that part of his life from her. If Katrina had known about his childhood then surely she wouldn't have asked him to help her now?

It was a relief when the phone suddenly rang because he wasn't sure that he was up to dealing with thoughts like that right then. He got up to answer it, listening with a growing sense of disbelief to what the voice on the other end of the line had to say. He hung up and turned to Luke, who was watching him expectantly.

'There's been another pile-up on the motorway, would you believe? They've called in all off-duty staff. From what I can gather, it's almost as bad as the one we dealt with the other night, so we'd better get going.'

He suddenly realised that he was still holding the little boy in his arms and frowned in consternation. 'What on earth am I going to do with Tomàs?'

'Just ease the lower end of the bone forward…a bit more… Perfect!'

Morgan nodded his satisfaction as Robin White, who was assisting him, successfully lined up the two ends of broken bone. It was one a.m. and he had been in Theatre for a little over four hours. Luke was in Theatre two and Armand St Juste, the French-Canadian exchange surgeon, was dealing with some of the less complex work in Theatre three. With a bit of luck they would be finished in another hour

but he was too experienced to discount the fact that the
unexpected could still happen.

He turned his attention back to the young woman on the
operating table. Frankly, Sandra Sullivan was lucky to be
alive. Her sternum, or breastbone as it was more commonly
known, had been fractured and the broken ends had come
within a millimetre of puncturing her heart. It had taken
some particularly skilful surgery to manipulate the two ends
of bone back into place but he was confident that the danger
point had passed.

He made a careful check that no fragments of bone had
sheared off but it was a clean break, the sternum snapped
in two by the force of the impact as the patient's chest had
rammed into the steering-wheel of her car. He swiftly set
about securing the fracture then closed the incision, layer
by layer, glancing at Robin as he neared the end of the
process.

'Fancy doing the last set of staples? It will be good practice for you.'

Robin eagerly accepted although Morgan stayed close at
hand in case of any problems. However, he was pleased
with the young houseman's work and said so as they left
Theatre a short time later.

'That was excellent work tonight, Robin. You seem to
have a natural aptitude for this type of surgery. You should
consider specialising in orthopaedics.'

'Thank you, sir!'

Robin beamed with delight at the compliment although
Morgan couldn't help but notice the surprise in the younger
man's eyes. It made him wonder if he had been a little lax
in his praise of late. Everyone needed to be told when they
were doing a good job, so he made a note to do it more
often, then found his mind veering off at a tangent as it
struck him that the idea would never have crossed his mind
a day or so earlier. Had it been Katrina's re-entry into his
life that had made him take stock?

The thought was deeply unsettling. Morgan's lips thinned as he discarded the soiled gown and went to scrub up before the next patient arrived. He couldn't afford to let thoughts of Katrina intrude while he was working. However, it was proving surprisingly difficult not to think about her when she was right here in the hospital.

Was she asleep? he found himself wondering, using his elbows to turn on the taps over the sink. Maybe she was unable to sleep because she was in pain or worrying about what was going to happen to Tomàs? That would play on her mind, of course, and it didn't make him feel good to know that he could have allayed her fears so easily. But how could he agree to help her when he knew that it would be the wrong thing to do?

'Ready whenever you are, Dr Grey.'

He shut off the water and composed himself before he turned to the nurse who was waiting to help him glove up. He had to put his personal problems aside for now but at some point soon he was going to have to resolve this situation. The trouble was that he had a nasty feeling that it was going to be easier said than done!

Katrina couldn't sleep. There had been a lot of coming and going in the ward that night but she knew that it wasn't the cause of her restlessness. It was due partly to discomfort because her leg was throbbing but mainly to worry.

She couldn't stop worrying about how she was going to manage without any money coming in. Her meagre savings were already sorely depleted so how would she pay the rent on the flat and buy food for herself and Tomàs? How could she hope to find enough to pay the solicitor's fees? Even if Morgan refused to help her, she would still go ahead with the adoption and that would cost money, money she didn't have.

She'd been so relieved when she'd tracked Morgan down. When she'd discovered that he'd moved out of

London, she'd been terrified that she wouldn't be able to trace him. However, an old friend from the hospital where they'd both worked had told her that he'd moved to Dalverston. She'd come here to see him with the express intention of solving her problems, but all she'd succeeded in doing had been to add to them!

She closed her eyes again, knowing that it was important that she try to rest, but the rattle of a trolley coming down the ward made it impossible to sleep. She watched as the nurses transferred yet another patient into one of the hastily set-up beds. The ward was packed to bursting point and she didn't envy them the task of keeping on top of all that needed to be done that night, especially when they had patients as agitated as this one appeared to be.

'Dr Grey will be down shortly to see you,' one of the nurses whispered soothingly to the woman. 'He won't be long so try not to worry.'

Katrina felt her heart surge when she heard that. It had never occurred to her that she might see Morgan again that night even though she knew that staff had been recalled because of the accident. She glanced towards the doors as they opened with a soft swish and felt the blood start drumming through her veins when she saw him coming into the ward.

He was still wearing the green scrub suit he must have worn in Theatre and in the dim glow from the nightlights he looked big and imposing as he strode down the aisle between the beds. His dark hair was clinging damply to his skull and there were deep lines grooved either side of his mouth, but he still moved with the same air of power and authority that she remembered so well. Despite what had happened between them in the past, Katrina felt her heart thunder in acknowledgement of the power he still possessed to stir her senses.

He must have sensed her watching him because he glanced her way as he passed her bed. Katrina felt the drumming beat of her heart increase as their eyes locked for a moment that could have lasted no longer than a millisecond yet which felt like a lifetime to her.

What could she see in those deep green eyes as they stared at her? she wondered dizzily. What was he thinking and feeling? It was impossible to tell yet she felt shaken to the very depths of her soul when he moved on, as though for that moment their spirits had touched, bonded, found again the wonderful rapport they had known in the past. Maybe there was still a chance that they could work this out if they rediscovered the ability to communicate which had been lost during those last dreadful months of their marriage.

Hope seemed to drain what little strength she had left and she closed her eyes, hearing the soft burr of Morgan's voice in the background as he spoke to the woman in the bed opposite hers. It was only when she gradually became aware that the sound had stopped that she opened her eyes and found him standing beside her.

'Can't you sleep?' he asked softly, his deep voice barely disturbing the silence that had fallen at last in the ward.

'It's been busy tonight,' she replied equally quietly, praying that he couldn't hear the ache in her voice. She wanted to reach out and touch him, forge a bond that was real and solid, not one that was fragile and easily broken, but she was afraid of making a mistake. It was one thing to hope that they might be able to recapture some of the closeness they had shared and something entirely different to know how to set about it.

'It has.' He sighed as he sank onto the edge of her bed and ran a weary hand round the back of his neck. 'It's the second such night we've had in the past week. I'm getting too old for all this. I feel absolutely worn out!'

She laughed softly, pleased that he felt able to unbend this much after what had happened earlier in the day. 'Rubbish! You're not old, Morgan. Well, not *that* old, anyway.'

He rolled his eyes expressively. 'I left myself wide open there, didn't I? You always did know how to put me in my place, Katrina Grey!'

'Someone had to take you down a peg or two,' she retorted, her spirits lifting as he responded in the same light vein. 'All I ever heard was how wonderful you were. I used to see housemen following in your wake when you did ward rounds with expressions of reverence on their faces. It's a wonder you didn't end up with an ego as big as a house!'

'There was no danger of that with you around!' His laughter was wryly amused. 'You made sure that I understood how unimpressed you were by me from the moment we met, as I recall.'

'Only because I was scared stiff that I was going to end up like everyone else,' she confessed.

'And that would have been a bad thing?' he asked, his brows arching.

'Oh, yes. I wanted to stand out from the crowd rather than merge with it. I wanted you to notice me, Morgan, not just see me as part of the furniture.'

'There was never any danger of that.' His voice had dropped, the husky sound of it sending a spasm along her nerves. Katrina felt her breath catch as she looked into his shadowy green eyes and saw the light that burned in their depths all of a sudden.

'Wasn't there?' she said shakily, every nerve straining as she waited for him to reply. Maybe it was silly to want him to admit how he had felt in those distant days, but she couldn't help it.

'No danger at all. As soon as I saw you, I knew that you were special.' He took a deep breath and even as she watched the light faded from his eyes. 'But all that was a long time ago, wasn't it? There's been a lot of water under the bridge since.'

He stood up abruptly and this time his tone was as cool

and indifferent as she had feared it would be. 'Anyway, you'd better get some sleep. Are you in pain? Do you need anything?'

'No, thank you. I'm fine.' She avoided his eyes, afraid that he would see how hurt she felt at the way he had summarily dismissed the past. Their life together was over and even though she had accepted that, it hurt to know that he could brush it aside with so little effort, such blatant disregard.

It was a moment before Katrina realised that he was still standing by the bed and it came as a surprise to see how uncomfortable he looked. Did he wish that he hadn't been quite so blunt, perhaps? Yet what point was there in either of them pretending? It would be far better for both of them if they were totally honest, no matter how much it might hurt.

'Tomàs is fine, by the way. I phoned my daily, Mrs Mackenzie, and she agreed to sleep over at the flat while I came into work.' He shrugged but she couldn't shake off the feeling that something was troubling him. 'Tomàs seems to like her so there's no need for you to worry about him.'

'I wasn't worried,' she said softly, refusing to let herself dwell on what might be wrong. Honesty was the best policy in this situation so she would stick to that. 'I know that you'll take the best possible care of him, Morgan. You're the one person in the whole world I trust completely with him.'

There was a moment when he seemed to be struggling to speak. Katrina watched myriad emotions cross his face before he suddenly bent and kissed her on the forehead. His lips were cool and the kiss lasted no more than a second, but she could feel ripples of heat spreading through her whole body, like the tiny after-shocks that followed in the wake of a seismic eruption.

He straightened abruptly, as though he was as shocked

by what he had done as she was, which was ridiculous really. Morgan *never* did anything on impulse! It wasn't in his nature to respond without due thought and consideration beforehand. Nevertheless, Katrina knew without the shadow of a doubt that on this occasion he had acted purely out of instinct.

'Try to get some sleep now,' he said brusquely, turning to leave.

'I shall. Goodnight, Morgan,' she whispered shakily, but he didn't reply. Perhaps he hadn't heard her or maybe he simply didn't trust himself not to say something that he might later regret.

The thought was so deliciously tantalising that she couldn't get it out of her head. It lingered at the edges of her consciousness as she drifted off to sleep.

It was funny how a simple 'maybe' could cause such mayhem.

CHAPTER FOUR

MORGAN was at his desk by eight the following morning. He had spent a sleepless night and it showed. The shadows under his eyes were a testament to the hours he'd spent tossing and turning whilst everything that had happened the previous day had raced through his head. It wasn't just the situation with Tomàs that had plagued him either. That kiss had caused him no end of grief because he still hadn't worked out *why* it had happened. However, he was at work now and he owed it to his patients to put aside his personal problems and focus on theirs.

He swept out of his office, frightening the life out of Robin, who was perched on the edge of Trisha Adams's desk, eating a doughnut. Morgan's mouth thinned with displeasure as he watched the young houseman frantically look around for somewhere to deposit the sugary confection.

'There is a bin under Mrs Adams's desk. I suggest you get rid of that pronto. And in future, please, make sure that you've had breakfast *before* you grace us with your presence, Dr White.'

'I...um... Sorry, sir.' Robin dropped the offending doughnut into the bin then hastily wiped his fingers on the tissue the secretary handed to him.

Morgan strode to the door, pretending that he hadn't seen the younger man draw his finger across his throat in a suitably expressive gesture. He didn't have time to indulge in puerile games neither did he expect his staff to indulge in them. Still, it wouldn't be fair to take out his irritation on Robin.

He scowled as he pressed the button and summoned the

lift. He didn't want to admit that he was irritated. He didn't want to admit that he felt *anything*! However, he could pretend all he liked but the truth was that what had happened last night had thrown him into turmoil. Damn Katrina for upsetting his nice, orderly world like this!

He stepped into the lift when it arrived, scowling as Robin scrambled in after him. 'I hope you're going to focus on the job today. We don't have room for slackers on this team. Orthopaedics is possibly the busiest department in the whole hospital and everyone needs to pull his weight.'

'I know that, sir. Sorry. And sorry about before.' Robin sighed as he pressed the button for the third floor. 'It won't happen again.'

'Make sure it doesn't,' Morgan replied, then instantly wished he could take back the words when he saw the abject expression that crossed the younger man's face.

An innate sense of fairness demanded that he should set matters straight. He turned to the younger man as they reached their floor. 'I apologise. It was unfair of me not to make allowances for the fact that you were here most of the night. What time did you manage to get to bed in the end?'

'Oh, around two, maybe a bit later.' Robin sounded a trifle stunned to be on the receiving end of an apology, but in his usual inimitable fashion he quickly rallied. 'It must have been even later when you got home, I imagine.'

'Just gone three. I may as well have stayed here and saved myself the journey for all the sleep I got, too.' He didn't elaborate as he opened the ward doors. Frankly, he was a bit surprised that he had said anything. It wasn't usual for him to pepper his conversation with personal remarks and it worried him that he should have done so that day.

He forced his mind back to the task at hand and nodded to Armand St Juste, who was leaning against the wall outside the office, yawning. 'Good morning, Armand. I see you made it in all right.'

'Just.' Armand gave one of his very expressive shrugs then fell into place beside Robin as Morgan swept into the ward. It was particularly busy in there that day with all the extra beds and the staff didn't appear to have noticed his arrival for once.

He shot an assessing look around, telling himself that he was taking stock but knowing that he was simply trying to control the urge to make straight for Katrina's bed. Luke Fabrizzi was off duty for the rest of the week so Morgan would be reviewing her case in his absence, but he couldn't in all conscience make her his first port of call, not if he wanted to avoid any unseemly gossip.

His gaze finally alighted on her bed and he felt an alarm bell go off inside his head when he saw that it was empty. For a moment the noise and bustle faded into a blur as panic assailed him. The thought that she might have been taken ill during the night sent a spasm of pure terror racing through him...

'Good morning.'

Morgan felt the colour drain from his face as he recognised her voice behind him. He spun round, ignoring the startled looks Robin and Armand exchanged. 'Are you all right?' he demanded, crouching down.

She was sitting in a wheelchair, her injured leg supported by the raised footrest. Her hair was wet, the honey-brown strands clinging to the shoulders of the towelling robe she was wearing. Morgan caught the scent of soap and talcum powder as he bent towards her, felt the damp warmth of her skin flowing towards him, and his heart shot into overdrive. Suddenly, in the middle of the busy hospital ward, all he could think about were all the other times when Katrina had come to him warm and damp from her morning shower.

'Yes, of course.' She gave a tinkly laugh but he could

see the flush that had stained her cheeks and knew that she was as startled by his response as the others had been. 'Why?'

A tide of colour swept up his own face as he realised that his reaction had been way over the top. He straightened abruptly, gritting his teeth as he felt embarrassment setting in. He wasn't used to making a spectacle of himself and didn't enjoy the experience.

'I wondered if there had been a problem during the night when I noticed that your bed was empty,' he explained crisply. How he managed to make his voice sound quite so aloof he had no idea, but he could tell how successful his efforts had been when he saw all the animation leave Katrina's face.

'Nurse Bosanko offered to help me take a shower,' she explained in a flat little monotone which cut him to the quick. 'You can't imagine how wonderful it felt.'

'I see,' he replied shortly, fixing his attention on the nurse because he was afraid of making an even bigger fool of himself. He desperately wanted to apologise to Katrina for his brusqueness but what was the point? It would be far better to aim for a degree of civility in their dealings rather than try to foster a friendship neither could possibly feel.

'Is this the first time that the patient has been out of bed for any prolonged period, Nurse?' he asked, wondering why his heart felt like lead as that thought sank home.

'Yes, sir,' the woman replied calmly, although he wasn't blind to the amusement in her dark eyes. It was obvious that Nurse Bosanko had noted his panicky reaction just now, as the other two had, and had put her own interpretation on it!

It was all he could do to hide his dismay but years of practice had honed his ability to disguise his feelings. 'Then may I suggest that you get her back to bed immediately?'

Beatrice inclined her head although he had a feeling that

it was less out of deference than a fear that she might say
something unwise. He turned away as Katrina was wheeled
down the ward, trying his best to ignore the speculation on
the younger doctors' faces.

'Right, gentlemen, shall we make a start? We have a very
busy day ahead of us, I warn you.'

He led the way to the first bed, ruthlessly putting aside
all thoughts except those related to work. Work had been
his salvation for the past four years and it would continue
to be his mainstay, his prop. He couldn't afford to let anything come between him and what really mattered…

Not even Katrina? a small voice whispered.

Morgan's mouth thinned. Definitely not!

An hour later, Morgan arrived at Sandra Sullivan's bed.
The ward round had taken an inordinate amount of time
that day despite the fact that he had been ruthless about
how long he'd spent at each patient's bedside. He hated
having to skimp on his time that way but he'd had no
choice. The sheer number of new patients had meant that
he'd had to cut corners wherever possible.

He glanced round as they gathered around Sandra
Sullivan's bed. Their numbers had been swelled by the ad-
dition of Cheryl Rothwell, his junior registrar, plus two
students from the local medical school. Sister Carter had
joined them as well and she had just finished updating them
on the patient's obs. Now it was time to discuss the operation that Sandra Sullivan had undergone the previous
night, and he had decided that the honour should fall to
Robin.

'Robin, if you'd care to take over and tell everyone what
happened in Theatre last night?'

He stepped aside as Robin began outlining the patient's
injuries at the time of admission. It gave him a chance to
draw breath after the past hectic hour, although he soon
began to wonder if that was a good thing when he found

his attention wandering. Katrina's bed was just across the aisle and he couldn't help but be aware of her presence.

He forced himself to focus on what Robin was saying, but all it took was the sound of Katrina's laughter to ruin his concentration again. He glanced over his shoulder and felt his pulse leap when he saw her smiling at the woman in the next bed. Her hair had dried now and the long strands fell smoothly around her face, catching the light each time she turned her head.

Morgan's hands clenched but even the pressure of his nails digging into his palms couldn't negate the tingle in his flesh as he recalled how wonderfully silky Katrina's hair had felt, how it had looked spread across the pillows when they'd made love…

'Dr Grey…sir?'

He blinked and everything shot back into focus. It was disconcerting to realise that everyone was looking expectantly at him. He cleared his throat, wishing that he'd paid more attention to what Robin had been saying. The thought of making a fool of himself twice in one day was more than he could stomach!

'Um, yes—' he began, only to be interrupted when Sandra Sullivan suddenly butted in.

'I have to get out of here, Doctor! Right away. I've already told the nurse that I want to leave but she said that I needed to speak to you. You have to understand that I can't stay here!'

Morgan frowned, forgetting his own problems when he heard the hysteria in the woman's voice. Sandra had been extremely agitated when she'd come round from the anaesthetic the previous night. She'd seemed very anxious about having to remain in hospital and had created such a fuss that the staff in the recovery room had asked him to have a word with her. He'd visited her in the ward and had done his best to make her understand how serious her condition was. However, it was obvious that she still didn't appreciate how important it was that she continue to receive proper medical care.

'You have just undergone major surgery, Ms Sullivan,' he explained firmly once more. 'To be blunt, you're extremely lucky to be alive. If your sternum had been driven inwards by just another millimetre then your heart would have been punctured. Whilst I am not anticipating any problems, there is always a risk after any surgery that something could go wrong. That's why it is vital that you should remain in hospital so that we can continue to monitor your progress.'

'But I can't stay! Don't you understand? I *have* to leave and you can't stop me!'

Sandra was becoming increasingly upset. Morgan just managed to bite back an oath when she tossed back the sheet and attempted to get out of bed. He was already moving forward when he heard her moan in pain before she collapsed back against the pillows.

'Lie still!' he ordered sternly, hurrying to her side. 'You aren't doing yourself any good by behaving like this. You'll only succeed in hampering your recovery.'

He turned to the ward sister as Sandra began to sob wretchedly. He had no idea why she was so anxious to leave, but that was the least of his worries at that moment. His main concern was to calm her down before she did herself any serious harm. 'Fetch me 10 mg of diazepam, please, Sister.'

Sister Carter hurried away and returned a few minutes later with the drug. He swiftly administered the injection to the sobbing woman then glanced at the group gathered around the bed. He could tell from their expressions that they were as bemused by the situation as he was and realised that he needed to do something about it. However, instinct told him that he might have a better chance of sorting things out if he spoke to Sandra on her own.

'I suggest we take a break now,' he told them crisply.

'Perhaps Sister would be kind enough to allow you to use the ward kitchen just this once? I'll expect you back here in ten minutes' time.'

He waited until they had trooped off down the ward then drew up a chair beside Sandra's bed and sat down. 'Can you tell what this is all about and why you're so anxious to leave, Ms Sullivan? If there's a problem at home, I'm sure we can do something about it. The hospital has its own team of social workers who would be happy to help you.'

Sandra wiped her eyes with the back of her hand. In other circumstances she would have been quite pretty, but pain and anxiety had etched deep lines on her face. 'I don't need help. I just want to get out of here.'

'I'm afraid that's out of the question at the moment,' he said firmly. 'As I've already explained, you will need to be closely monitored for the next week at least. After that then we can think about allowing you to go home so long as you have someone to take care of you.'

'A week!' Sandra exclaimed in dismay. He frowned when he heard real fear in her voice. 'But I can't stay here all that time! I just can't!'

'Why not? I'm sorry, Ms Sullivan, but I simply don't understand why it's so urgent that you leave. Can't you tell me?' He sighed when she shook her head. 'Then there's nothing I can do. All I can say is that anything you do tell me will be treated in the strictest confidence. If there's some sort of problem, I'm sure that we can sort it out.'

He paused, giving her a moment to reconsider, then stood up when she still didn't say anything. He couldn't force her to tell him what was wrong but it troubled him to see her looking so scared.

He patted her hand in an instinctive gesture of comfort then felt shock score through him when he realised what he had done. He had always cared about his patients but his concern had centred on their physical well-being more than anything else. It came as a surprise to find himself empathising with this woman and trying to understand why she was so afraid.

He turned away from the bed, feeling deeply unsettled all of a sudden. It didn't help when he found himself looking straight at Katrina. There was the beginning of a smile around her mouth and a warmth in her eyes that made an answering warmth flow through his veins.

Had Katrina seen what he'd done? he found himself wondering. And had it surprised her, too?

He had no idea but it threw him even further off balance to realise that she might have witnessed him behaving so out of character. It made him feel strangely vulnerable and that was the last thing he could afford to be at the present time. Four years ago he had sworn that he would never again lay himself open to heartache but how confident could he be of avoiding it now? Having Katrina back in his life was bound to have repercussions.

Katrina picked up a magazine as Morgan moved away but it was impossible to concentrate on its glossy pages. Witnessing his concern for the woman across the aisle had come as a shock and she couldn't deny it.

Oh, he had always been marvellous with his patients in the past, giving one hundred and ten per cent commitment when it came to their care. However, there had been a certain aloofness about the way he'd treated them, a distance which had been as natural to him as breathing. She couldn't recall having seen him try to connect with anyone as he'd tried to do with Sandra just now. For some reason it made her heart feel that bit lighter and gave her room to hope once again. Perhaps he would agree to her request after all?

The thought kept buzzing around her head so that she was a mass of nerves by the time the group arrived at her bed. Morgan nodded politely to her then turned to the students.

'Mrs Grey is Dr Fabrizzi's patient, but in his absence I shall be supervising her care.' He quickly explained what had been done to repair her femur, then answered a question from one of the students about the type of nails that had been used to fix the bone together.

Unlike a lot of consultants, who found supervising students a tiresome nuisance, Morgan never begrudged the time he spent explaining the most minor points. However, Katrina found herself becoming increasingly irritated as he went into detail about the choice of closed intramedullary locked nails for her operation without ever once looking at her. It wasn't pleasant to feel that she was being deliberately ignored!

She glowered up at him when he paused, her hazel eyes sparkling with temper when they met his cool green ones. 'It sounds as though you might be considering writing a paper on me, Dr Grey. I wonder if my case is worth a mention in *The Lancet*?'

'That will be for Dr Fabrizzi to decide,' he replied with the coolest of smiles. 'You're his patient and I wouldn't dream of pre-empting him.'

'Of course. But as head of surgery you have overall charge of all the patients, don't you?' She smiled sweetly at him, refusing to be put in her place by his chilly attitude, such a sharp contrast to the concern he'd shown Sandra not long before.

'That is correct. Ultimately, I am in charge of everything that goes on in the surgical wards.' His tone was polite to a fault and totally at odds with the searing look he gave her.

Katrina managed to hide her smile when she realised that he was annoyed even if he was doing his best to disguise it. It gave her a perverse sort of pleasure to realise that she'd managed to needle him. That would teach him to ignore her!

She realised that he was still speaking and quickly marshalled her thoughts, feeling some of her satisfaction evaporate when she heard the aloof note in his voice.

'Fortunately, it is rare that I ever need to intervene in a patient's care and I'm certainly not expecting to have to do so in this instance. Dr Fabrizzi will continue to be in charge of your case until you leave us.'

With that he moved away, the rest of the party following meekly in his wake. Katrina didn't even pause to think about what she was doing as she stuck out her tongue at his back. It was just unfortunate that he happened to glance round at that moment to reply to something Cheryl had said, and saw her action.

Katrina saw a flash of something cross his face but he was too far away for her to tell what it was. She lowered her eyes, feeling her cheeks burning as she realised how childish it had been. Anyone would think she was nine, not a grown woman of twenty-nine!

She looked up as a shadow fell over her, feeling her heart starting to pound when she realised that he had come back. She could tell at once that he was annoyed and knew that he had every right to be. It had been unforgivable to behave that way in front of his colleagues.

'I'm sorry. It was a very childish thing to do,' she said before he could speak.

'At least you realise that,' he replied repressively. 'Look, Katrina, I know how difficult this situation is, but it would help if we at least managed to maintain a little dignity in our dealings with each other.'

'I know and you're right. It's just that...' She broke off, realising what she had been about to say and how it would have sounded. How *pathetic* to admit that she'd resented the fact that he'd been so kind to Sandra when he'd ignored her!

'Just what?' he prompted. He sighed when she shook her head. 'Come on, tell me what you were going to say.' He gave a soft laugh that brought her eyes flying to his face and she was shocked by the amusement she saw on it. 'It isn't like you to prevaricate. You used to come right out and say what you thought, and to hell with the consequences!'

'Maybe I've grown up.' She grimaced as his brows rose. 'And maybe not. All right, then, if you want the truth, I was annoyed by the way you deliberately ignored me just now.'

'Ignored you?'

She heard the surprise in his voice and sighed. 'Yes. You stood there rattling off all the facts about my operation and totally ignored me. It...well, it just hurt.'

'I didn't realise....' He stopped and she saw an expression of weariness cross his face. 'I did, didn't I? My only excuse is that I didn't do it consciously. It was a kind of reflex action, I suppose.'

'Reflex action? What do you mean by that?'

'A knee-jerk reaction, a gut response.' His tone was wry when he saw that she didn't understand. 'What I'm trying to say, Katrina, is that I find this situation extremely difficult to deal with. That's probably why I can't seem to find the right balance.'

She couldn't recall him ever having been so open about his feelings before so the admission touched her all the more deeply. 'And I'm not making it any easier by behaving like a silly child, am I?'

She brushed her fingers over the back of his hand in a gesture of apology then quickly withdrew them when it struck her that she had no right to do that.

'I never meant to make this so difficult for you, Morgan. I want you to believe that,' she whispered, hoping that he could hear that she was telling the truth.

'It was bound to have been difficult for both of us, Katrina,' he said quietly. 'You want something from me that I'm not prepared to give.'

'Even though you'll be denying a little boy a secure future?'

Maybe it was the wrong time to try and press home her point but she had no choice when she heard the finality in his voice. The thought that he might have made up his mind not to help her scared her. She had to find a way to make him see that they needed to talk before he made his final decision!

'Don't exaggerate, Katrina,' he said stiffly. He glanced over his shoulder to where the others were waiting for him to join them and sighed. 'Anyway, this is certainly not the time to talk about it.'

'Then when can we talk about it?' she demanded. She gave a sharp laugh because she suspected that he was simply trying to fob her off. 'I'm available any time you care to choose because I'm certainly not going anywhere, so you tell me when it *would* be convenient!'

'This afternoon, then. I'm in Theatre for the rest of the morning but I should be through by one. I'll come back then so that we can get this sorted out once and for all.'

His expression was sombre. 'However, I'm warning you, Katrina, that I won't change my mind. I will not be coerced into doing something I know for a fact would be wrong!'

He walked away without another word. Katrina sank back against the pillows and closed her eyes. Her heart was beating so fast that it felt as though it was going to explode, but she had to calm down. Before Morgan came back she had to work out exactly how she was going to convince him to help her.

Panic rose inside her as she recalled how once before she'd tried to persuade him not to take a particular course of action. She'd tried desperately to make him see what a mistake it would be to end their marriage, but he'd refused to listen to her pleas. It didn't seem like a particularly good omen but she couldn't afford to dwell on it now. This time it wasn't just herself and Morgan who would get hurt if he refused to see sense. She had to think about what it would mean for Tomàs. That was the reason she had come to Dalverston in the first place.

Had it been the *only* reason, though? her conscience whispered. Had she come to see Morgan *purely* to safeguard the child's future?

Katrina closed her mind to the insidious little voice. She couldn't afford to get sidetracked by thoughts like that. It was Tomàs who mattered. Nobody else!

CHAPTER FIVE

MORGAN'S last operation of the morning was without doubt the most complex. The patient, a man in his thirties called Graham Walker, had fallen during a recent skiing holiday and had fractured two of the bones in his right wrist. It was the type of injury that frequently caused problems at a later date by seriously restricting a patient's hand movements. What made it more difficult in this instance was the fact that Graham Walker was a professional cellist and needed to regain full mobility in his wrist.

Morgan studied the X-rays again. He could see that of the eight wrist bones, arranged in two rows, one row articulating with the bones in the forearm and the other connecting with the bones in the palm, Graham had managed to break a bone from each row, which presented even more of a challenge. Not only was there a danger of his wrist movement being restricted but also that he might have problems using his thumb. There was no doubt in Morgan's mind that the operation was going to be complicated but it was the sort of test of his skills which he enjoyed.

He returned to the operating table and glanced at Dave Carson, who was his anaesthetist that day. 'How are we doing?'

'Ready when you are,' Dave replied laconically. His laid-back attitude belied the fact that he was one of the best anaesthetists in the country. Morgan was always pleased when he saw Dave's name on the roster because he knew that he could be confident that things would run smoothly.

'Scalpel,' he said quietly, suddenly eager to get started.

The theatre sister slapped the razor-sharp blade into his palm and he made the first incision. Although many doctors would have treated a fracture like this with a simple cast, he was concerned about possible tendon damage. He nodded when he opened the synovial sheath, the protective capsule which surrounded the tendons, and saw that his suspicions had been correct. The tendon connecting the man's forearm and thumb was torn and would need repairing.

It was extremely delicate work and he was very conscious that he could do a great deal of harm if he wasn't careful. If he made the repair too tight, that would also restrict movement. He worked swiftly and deftly, not speaking except to issue brief instructions to various members of his team. Unlike a lot of surgeons, he preferred peace and quiet while he was operating, and his staff respected that. However, by the time he was round to closing the incision, he was pleased with what he had achieved. Graham Walker had an excellent chance of playing his cello again.

'Thank you, everyone. That was a good morning's work.' He clapped Dave on the shoulder as he passed, earning himself a deceptively sleepy grin. It was good to know that the people he worked with were as dedicated as he was, he thought as he left the theatre.

Shedding his cap and gown in the bin outside the door, he headed straight for the locker room and hurriedly showered. He dressed quickly, frowning when he realised that it was already half past one. He had a meeting with the hospital's manager at two and wasn't sure if he would have time to visit Katrina beforehand. Maybe he should send a message to her, explaining that he wouldn't be able to keep their appointment after all.

'Dr Grey?' Aileen Roberts, the sister in charge of Theatre that day, gave a cursory knock then poked her head round the door. 'Message for you from Roger Hopkins's secretary to say that this afternoon's meeting has been cancelled. She didn't say why.'

'Right. Thanks.'

Morgan sighed as Aileen hurried away. He was uncomfortably aware that he had been using the meeting as an excuse to delay having to speak to Katrina. It wasn't like him to be so faint-hearted but he wasn't looking forward to it. He didn't want to have to hurt her by refusing again to do as she'd asked, but what choice did he have? There was no way on earth that he could agree to this ridiculous plan!

He whipped up his indignation, hoping that it would help him deal with what was to come. He made his way to the ward and went straight to Katrina's bed, seeing the lines of strain around her eyes and mouth. It was obvious that she was worried sick about what he was going to say, but he resisted the urge to reassure her. He wouldn't lie and lead her to believe that he would do as she wanted him to do. That would be too cruel.

'You've made up your mind, haven't you, Morgan?' she said quietly, her hazel eyes holding his as he sat down.

'Yes.' He took a deep breath but it didn't make it any easier to say what had to be said, to witness her pain when he told her his decision. His only aim had always been to protect her yet he was bitterly aware of how badly he had failed. All he could do now was to get this over with as fast as possible.

'I can't help you, Katrina. It wouldn't be right—not for Tomàs, not for you and certainly not for me.'

She closed her eyes as though the words were too painful to absorb. Morgan's hands clenched because the urge to offer some shred of comfort was overwhelming. However, he knew in his heart that he was doing the right thing and that one day she would be glad that he had refused to help her. When she met someone else, a man whom she could love as she had once loved him, then she would look back at this moment with relief. There would be no ghosts from her past to deal with, just the future to look forward to, a future with this other man and Tomàs, and possibly their own children as well.

The thought was like a dagger through his heart, so painful that for a moment he wasn't sure that he could bear it. It took every scrap of self-control to hide his feelings when she opened her eyes and looked at him.

'Isn't there anything I can say to make you reconsider? I *know* you're making a mistake, Morgan. I just don't know how to make you understand that!'

His anger rose on a great wave, fed by feelings he had no right to feel. It wasn't fair to have ended their marriage yet feel angry at the thought of the life she might lead with another man.

'And I don't understand why you are so arrogant as to believe that it *is* a mistake. What gives you the right to pass judgement on me, Katrina?' His tone was harsh and he saw her flinch but pain and anger drove him on. 'Who appointed you as the expert on how I should lead my life?'

'Nobody, and I wouldn't dream of making such a claim either.' She met his gaze proudly, her hazel eyes spitting fire back at him. Morgan felt a stirring in the pit of his stomach as he realised that she wasn't deterred by his anger. Of all the people he had ever known, Katrina had been the only one who had refused to back down when he'd tried to freeze her out. Her spirit was one of the things he'd loved most about her.

His anger drained away as swiftly as it had arisen, and he sighed. 'I'm sorry. That was uncalled-for.'

'It was but I accept your apology.' There was a hint of laughter in her voice that brought his eyes to her face, and he frowned when he saw that she was trying hard not to laugh.

'What's so funny?' he demanded incredulously, wishing that he could find anything the least bit amusing about the situation.

'You. Me. Us.' Her tone was warm, teasing. It stirred an instant response inside him which he immediately resented.

'Well, I'm glad that you find it all so amusing...' he began, only to stop when she gave an exasperated groan.

'Oh, no, you don't. You're not going all stern and stuffy on me, Morgan Grey. I know your tactics and they won't work. I'm not letting you shut me out because this is too important.'

She reached across the bed and grasped his hand. 'If you won't think about me or yourself then think about Tomàs and what you can do for him. Wouldn't you like to know that his future is assured after everything he's been through?'

'Of course I would! However, I don't believe that Tomàs's future hinges solely on my agreement to help you adopt him. And I refuse to let you emotionally blackmail me into doing what you want,' he retorted, withdrawing his hand out of her reach. 'I'm sorry, but that's my final decision. I won't change my mind. Getting involved in this would be a mistake and that's the end of the matter.'

She shrugged. 'Fine. If that's how you feel then I won't waste your time any further. I know what a busy man you are, Morgan, so I won't detain you.' She picked up a magazine, studiously ignoring him as she flicked through its pages.

He stood up abruptly, feeling somewhat at a loss. Maybe he should have felt pleased that she had accepted his decision but he felt more surprised than anything else. Was that really the end of the affair?

He took a couple of steps away from the bed then stopped and looked back, overwhelmed by a feeling of indecision which he couldn't recall having experienced before. Katrina just carried on reading, her silky hair falling forward so that he couldn't see her face. To all intents and purposes it appeared that she had given up trying to per-

suade him, but it left him feeling more anxious than relieved, funnily enough.

Surely there were other things they needed to discuss, he
thought, like how she was going to manage in the coming
months. It wouldn't be easy to look after Tomàs with her
leg in plaster, plus there was the question of how she was
going to manage financially when she wouldn't be able to
work.

They might have solved one problem but there were an
awful lot more that still needed sorting out, as far as he
could see!

Katrina kept her eyes firmly on the magazine. She knew
that Morgan was still standing by her bed but she refused
to look up. Maybe it had been a mistake not to try and
persuade him but that comment about emotional blackmail
had struck a particularly painful chord. How could it be
right to *force* him to do something that he might only regret?

He suddenly sat down again and there was no way that
she could stop herself looking at him then. There were
shadows in his eyes and an unaccustomed air of uncertainty
about him that made her heart ache. Morgan was finding
this situation extremely stressful and it didn't make her feel
good to know that it was all her fault.

'Whilst we might have resolved the adoption issue,
there's a few other things which we need to sort out,' he
said flatly.

'Are there?' She smiled thinly, trying to push the thought
that she had been wrong to come to Dalverston to the back
of her mind. She'd done what she'd thought necessary and
there was no point in wishing that she'd handled the situation differently.

'I'm not sure that I understand what you mean,' she began, then felt her breath catch as a sudden, unpalatable
thought struck her. 'Was that your way of telling me that
you want a divorce, by any chance?'

'Not at all, although I suppose we shall need to talk about that at some stage.' He shrugged when she looked at him. 'You might want to get married again one day, Katrina. It would be easier to get the formalities out of the way now rather than complicate matters in the future.'

'It's not something I've thought about,' she said quietly, struggling to keep the ache out of her voice. It was foolish to get upset at the thought of officially ending their marriage, but she couldn't help it.

She took a deep breath and hurried on, determined not to let him see how the idea had affected her. 'Anyway, I'm more concerned with the present rather than what may or may not happen in the future.'

'Which is what I'm worried about, too,' he said bluntly. 'How are you going to manage when you leave here? It won't be easy, looking after Tomàs on your own. It's going to take months for your leg to heal.'

'I know that.' She shrugged although she knew that it was a valid point. Caring for a lively three-year-old was extremely hard work even without a broken leg! 'I'll cope somehow. Don't worry about it.'

'I can't just ignore the problem. For heaven's sake, Katrina, I'm not some sort of a monster who doesn't give a damn what happens to you and the child!' he replied harshly.

'I know that, Morgan. And I appreciate your concern, really I do. It's just that I'm used to coping on my own so I'll manage somehow.'

She heard the quaver in her voice and bit her lip. Despite her assertions, she couldn't help worrying how she was going to deal with the everyday problems like cooking and shopping, for instance. It would be months before she would be fully mobile again and she could imagine the difficulties she was going to encounter only too easily.

He sighed heavily. 'And you'll also manage to go out to work, will you? Unless you happen to have won the lottery,

I assume that you'll still need to earn a living. Will you be able to do that when you can't walk, Katrina?'

'I have a little money put by…' she began, then realised that there was no point in lying when she saw the scepticism on his face. For one thing she had never been good at it and for another Morgan had always been able to read her like an open book.

That last thought was oddly disquieting but she put it out of her head while she concentrated on more pressing problems. 'I don't know how I'm going to manage about money, if you want the truth. I had been hoping to start work for a nursing agency once I'd made arrangements for Tomàs's care. It seemed like the best option because then I'd be able to choose what hours I worked. However, that's all gone by the board now. As for savings, well, I used up most of what I had for the deposit on our flat in Derby.'

'Derby? So that's where you decided to settle.' He frowned. 'Why there?'

'I used to live there as a small child and I have a lot of happy memories of the place. Now that Mum and Dad have gone over to New Zealand to be near my sister Zoë and her family, it didn't really matter where I chose.' She shrugged. 'Anyway, what made you decide to move to Dalverston? I can't recall you mentioning that you had links to this area.'

'I don't.' His tone was clipped. 'That was its main attraction, in fact. It's worked out extremely well, too.'

'I see.' Katrina looked away, because she *did* see. She understood only too well why Morgan had made the decision to leave London. She took a deep breath but the pain was inching towards her heart once again. He had wanted to cut all ties with the past so that he could erase her from his life.

There was a moment when neither of them said anything before he glanced at his watch. 'I'll have to go, but I want you to know that I shall help you any way I can, Katrina.

I don't want you worrying yourself to death about how you're going to manage.'

'Thank you.' There was nothing else she could think of to say and she saw him frown. Had he heard that ache in her voice, the faint but unmistakable hint of despair? Morgan's offer of help had been a genuine one but he didn't seem to realise that she could put up with any hardship rather than face the fact that he would never do the one thing she really wanted him to do for her.

He stood up abruptly and there was a touch of impatience in his voice when he spoke, which she didn't understand. 'I'll bring Tomàs in to see you tonight. Is there anything that you need?'

She shook her head. 'No, thank you. How is Tomàs? He's not causing you too much trouble, I hope?'

'Not at all. He's been as good as gold, apart from last night.' He shrugged when she looked at him. 'He was very clingy when I got in, wouldn't let me put him down. Luke suggested that he might have sensed that I was upset...'

He stopped and she saw the shutters come down over his face. 'Anyway, he was back to his usual lively self this morning.'

'Good. He's normally a very easygoing child and very friendly with people he likes,' she said softly, trying not to let him see how that comment had affected her. Morgan had been upset because of her and it made her feel wretched to know that.

'Don't!' He tilted her chin so that she was forced to look at him and she saw the concern in his eyes. 'Stop blaming yourself, Katrina. It wasn't your fault that I was on edge yesterday.'

'No?' She gave a sceptical laugh. 'Then whose fault was it? If I hadn't come here to ask you to help me, none of this would have happened, would it? You wouldn't be having to look after Tomàs, I wouldn't be stuck in this bed and *neither* of us would be having our emotions put through the wringer!'

He smiled at that so that the stern lines of his face softened all of a sudden. 'You're probably guilty of unleashing fire and plague, not to mention famine on the world as well. Why not add those to your list of sins while you're at it?'

'Why not?' She couldn't help smiling at his teasing. 'They are probably all down to me, if the truth be told!'

'Rubbish! You only did what you thought was right,' he said firmly.

'So long as you understand that,' she replied softly. 'I never meant to hurt you, Morgan.'

'I know.' His grip tightened for a second before he let her go. 'I'll see you tonight, then. Try to get some rest this afternoon. Promise?'

'I promise,' she whispered.

She sank back against the pillows after he had left, and took a deep breath. Morgan had made his decision and she had to respect it. It wasn't going to be easy because she'd been pinning her hopes on him helping her even though she'd known all along that he might refuse. Now she had to look to the future. That Morgan would play no part in it was something she had to get used to. After all, she'd had four years to come to terms with the idea so it shouldn't be that difficult to do.

She sighed. There were no guarantees, though.

The day came to an end at last. Morgan drove home and parked in the underground garage beneath the block of luxury flats where he lived. He'd been fortunate to find such excellent accommodation when he'd moved to Dalverston because there wasn't an abundance of suitable property in the town.

Green-belt regulations meant that building work was strictly controlled, but this small development of luxury apartments had been built specifically for the growing num-

ber of high earners who had moved to the area. A new
business park, which had been built just outside the town's
boundaries, had attracted a lot of interest from various mul-
tinational corporations and their key staff had needed suitable accommodation.

The new development had had an impact on the hospital
as well as on the local economy, and had been one of the
reasons why he had decided to take the post as head of
surgery. Dalverston General had been declared a centre of
excellence for a number of specialities, surgery being one
of them.

Morgan had the satisfaction of knowing that the work he
and his colleagues were doing was leading the field in many
areas, and he'd never regretted moving out of London.
However, as he let himself into the flat, he found himself
wondering if he would have made the decision if he and
Katrina hadn't parted. It was strange to think that something good had come out of such a painful episode in his
life.

'Papa!'

He dropped his brief case as Tomàs came rushing along
the hall and hurled himself at him. Scooping the child into
his arms, he tossed him into the air, smiling when he heard
the little boy's delighted squeals. It was a routine they had
slipped into over the past few days—Tomàs would come
running to greet him and they'd have a few minutes of wild
play, although it suddenly occurred to him that he enjoyed
it every bit as much as the child did. He would miss this
when Katrina took the little boy home to Derby.

The thought was more than a little unsettling. He made
a conscious effort to put it out of his mind for the simple
reason that he didn't know how to deal with it. Perching
Tomàs on his shoulders, he headed for the kitchen where
Mrs Mackenzie was waiting to greet him. A motherly
woman in her sixties, who still retained the lilting accent
of her native Scotland, she had been an absolute godsend

in the past few days and he didn't know how he would have coped without her help.

'I'll be off, then, Dr Grey,' she said, taking her coat off the back of a chair. 'Thomas has had his tea and there's a casserole in the oven to save you having to cook for yourself.'

'That's very kind of you, Mrs Mackenzie,' Morgan told her warmly, putting the little boy down. 'I really appreciate all your help. I don't know how I would have managed if you hadn't stepped into the breach.'

'Och, it's my pleasure.' She bent and held out her arms to the child. 'Don't I get a goodbye kiss, then, laddie?'

Tomàs rushed to her and planted a noisy kiss on her lined cheek. 'Kiss,' he repeated proudly.

'That's right. Clever boy!' Mrs Mackenzie gave him a hug then picked up her bag. 'He's a fast learner. It won't be long before he's speaking English as well as you and me. Anyway, same time tomorrow, is it, Doctor?'

'Please.'

Morgan saw her out then turned as Tomàs tugged on his hand. The little boy broke into a torrent of rapid Spanish, obviously trying to tell him about something that had happened during the day. The only word Morgan could understand was 'Mama' although he tried his best to follow what the child was saying. Tomàs obviously realised that he didn't understand because he started tugging Morgan towards the sitting-room.

He laughed as he allowed himself to be led into the room and saw the picture lying on the coffee-table. 'Oh, so you've drawn me another picture, have you? Let's take a look, then.'

He picked up the sheet of paper, feeling a sudden tightening in his chest when he saw what the little boy had drawn. He didn't need Tomàs's explanation to understand what it was meant to represent.

'Papa, Mama y Tomàs.' The child pointed to each of the

stick figures in turn, smiling proudly as he did so. *'Somos una familia! Sí?'*

Morgan took a deep breath but the pain didn't ease even the tiniest bit. It seemed to be snaking around his heart, squeezing tighter and tighter. *Somos una familia*—we are a family—yet that was the one thing they could never be...

Unless he changed his mind and agreed to help Katrina adopt the little boy.

The thought slid in before he could stop it and he was hard-pressed to conceal his dismay. He didn't want to start having doubts but suddenly it wasn't easy to rid himself of the thought that he might have made a mistake.

'Papa?'

He looked down as Tomàs slid his warm little hand into his, feeling his heart swelling with a wealth of emotions he had never experienced before. It was a mixture of tenderness laced with an overwhelming desire to protect this child for the rest of his days. It was the most altruistic mix of emotions and yet the most dangerous. He couldn't simply rationalise it away, neither could he ignore it. For the first time in his adult life he knew that all he had to fall back on was instinct, and the idea scared him half to death.

It felt as though he were walking along a tightrope without a safety net to catch him if he fell!

CHAPTER SIX

KATRINA soon discovered that being a patient was a whole new experience, a world removed from the time she had spent working on the wards of one of London's busiest hospitals. Then there had never seemed to be enough hours in a day to get through all the work that had needed doing whereas now the time seemed to drag.

By the time Friday came around she was starting to chafe at the restrictions her injured leg imposed on her. It didn't help when a promised physiotherapy session had to be cancelled because the therapist had gone home sick. She simply wasn't used to sitting around all day! She must have been looking particularly fed up because Beatrice stopped by her bed and put her hands on her hips.

'So what's wrong with you, my girl? You'll turn the milk sour with a face like that.'

Katrina sighed glumly. 'I'm bored, that's all. I'm not used to having nothing to do.'

'I don't expect you had a minute to yourself when you were working with those poor little kiddies,' Beatrice observed sympathetically.

Beatrice had asked Katrina about her work in South America and had seemed genuinely interested in everything that she'd heard. Katrina knew that the situation between Morgan and herself was still causing a lot of interest amongst the staff so she'd been circumspect about what she'd said. However, she had seen no reason to lie when Beatrice had asked her about Tomàs, and had explained that she was hoping to legalise his adoption with the British authorities. What people made of Morgan's involvement in her plans was up to them.

'I certainly didn't,' she agreed ruefully. 'The days weren't long enough to fit everything in! I used to fall into bed at night completely exhausted. The one luxury I yearned for most while I was there was sleep!'

'I know how that feels, believe me.' Beatrice chuckled. 'My little one is teething and I can't remember the last time I had a full night's sleep. Simon and I are like zombies most of the time. He told me last night that he fell asleep at his desk yesterday. He only woke up when his secretary came to see why he wasn't answering his phone!'

'The joys of parenthood,' Katrina declared with a smile. 'At least Tomàs is past that stage now, thank heavens.'

'It's all downhill from here on,' Beatrice assured her. 'Anyway, instead of sitting there moping, how do you fancy doing something for me?'

'Of course. What do you want me to do?' She shot a rueful look at her plastered leg and sighed. 'I'm a bit limited, though.'

'That's not a problem. What I need you to do can be done sitting down.' Beatrice glanced across the aisle then lowered her voice. 'Do you think you could have a go at finding out what's wrong with Sandra Sullivan? We've all tried to get her to tell us why she's so eager to leave but she just clams up. It sounds daft but I have a feeling that something isn't right about that situation.'

'She does seem very keyed up,' Katrina agreed quietly, looking at the other woman.

Sandra was sitting in a chair beside her bed. She had a magazine on her lap but it was obvious that she wasn't reading it. She looked round when the ward doors opened and Katrina was shocked by the expression of fear that crossed Sandra's face before she realised that it was just one of the ward cleaners arriving.

'A few of the other patients have tried talking to her,' she explained, turning to Beatrice again. 'But Sandra has cut them dead so that's why nobody bothers with her now.'

'You can't blame them, can you? Nobody likes being ignored. That's why I thought you'd be the best person to help.' Beatrice grinned broadly. 'We nurses soon develop a thick skin so *you'll* not take offence if she tries to cut you down to size!'

Katrina laughed. 'That's a backhanded compliment if ever I heard one! But I'll give it a go if you think I might be able to help...' She stopped as Sandra got up at that moment and slowly left the ward. 'Looks like I might have missed my chance, I'm afraid.'

'She's probably gone to the day room—she spends a lot of time in there,' Beatrice said quickly. 'How do you fancy a change of scene? I could pop you in a wheelchair and take you down there.'

'Why not? It will give me a breather even if it doesn't achieve anything else,' she agreed readily, glad of the distraction.

The nurse fetched a wheelchair and helped her get settled, using the leg rest to support the weighty cast. There were several patients already in the day room, watching television, although Katrina couldn't help noticing that Sandra had chosen a seat well away from everyone else. She found herself wondering how much success she would have in getting through to Sandra when it was obvious that the woman didn't want to talk to anyone. However, she was there now so she may as well give it a go.

Beatrice wheeled the chair over to where Sandra was sitting by the window and set the brake. 'Right, ladies, I'll leave you two to introduce yourselves.'

Katrina cleared her throat as the nurse disappeared. She was very conscious of the fact that Sandra hadn't looked at her. It was obvious that the woman intended to ignore her in the hope that she would go away, but she wasn't going to be deterred so easily.

'Hi, I'm Katrina Grey. I'm in the bed opposite you.'

'I know.' Sandra still didn't look at her, her gaze locked

on the view from the window. Katrina frowned when she saw how strained the other woman looked.

Sandra couldn't have been more than thirty-five yet there was a dejected air about her that made her appear much older than that. Obviously she must have been still in some discomfort from her recent surgery, but Katrina suspected that it wasn't the real cause of her problems. All of a sudden she realised that she wanted to get to the bottom of the mystery.

'It's a bit of a drag, being stuck in hospital, isn't it?' she said conversationally. 'I don't know about you but I find that the days seem never-ending. I suppose it's because I'm normally so busy. I'm a nurse, by the way. What do you do?'

'Nothing.'

Sandra's curt tone would have discouraged most people, but it simply heightened Katrina's curiosity. She found herself wondering why the woman seemed so determined to rebuff any friendly overtures. In a funny sort of way, Sandra's attitude reminded her of how Morgan had responded when they'd first met—he'd been deliberately offhand at first although she hadn't let it deter her. She had known from the beginning how important it was that she should get to know him better.

The thought created a feeling of warmth in the pit of her stomach but she resolutely ignored it because it wasn't the right time to think about such things. She gave a light laugh and saw Sandra look at her in surprise. 'Nothing? You mean that you don't have a job or that you are that rare breed, a lady of leisure?'

'I don't have a job,' Sandra replied reluctantly, forced into either answering the question or being downright rude by ignoring it. 'But I do keep busy in the house. M-my husband is very particular and likes the place to look just so when he comes home from work.'

'Oh, I see,' Katrina replied, trying to hide her surprise

because she'd had no idea that Sandra was married. As far
as she could recall, the woman hadn't had a single visitor
during the whole time she'd been in the ward. She found
herself wondering what had happened to Sandra's husband
and if his absence was the reason for her strange behaviour.
If Sandra and her husband had recently split up, for instance, that could certainly explain it. Hadn't she found it
difficult to cope after she and Morgan had parted?

The thought that the woman might be suffering the same
kind of anguish that she had gone through immediately
touched her heart, and made her all the more determined
to help if she could.

'I haven't noticed your husband visiting you,' she observed gently. 'Has he had problems getting to the hospital?'

'He's abroad on business,' Sandra replied in a strained
voice.

'Oh, what a shame! Won't his firm allow him to fly
home? That seems a bit harsh in the circumstances,' she
exclaimed sympathetically, thinking that it was no wonder
the poor soul was so upset.

Sandra shook her head and her eyes were a little wild
all of a sudden. 'He doesn't know...about the accident, I
mean.'

'Why ever not?' Katrina frowned when she saw Sandra's
hands clench. She had no idea what was going on but it
was obvious that the woman was extremely distressed.
'Look, if you've had problems contacting him then the police should be able to help...'

'No! I don't want anyone telling him what's happened.
Don't you understand? That's the last thing I need!' Sandra
stood up abruptly. 'I know you're only trying to be kind
but you don't understand. Anthony will be furious when he
finds out!'

'No, I don't understand,' she began, but Sandra didn't

wait to hear what she had to say as she hurried from the room.

Katrina sighed as she manoeuvred her wheelchair to the door and watched the other woman hurrying back to the ward. She had a horrible feeling that she might have made matters worse rather than better, and that was the last thing she'd wanted to do.

'Why the long face?'

She looked round in surprise, feeling her heart give a small jolt of pleasure when she saw Morgan coming along the corridor. Luke had conducted the ward round that day so it was the first she'd seen of him. She couldn't help but feel her spirits lift even though she knew how foolish it was to react that way.

'I think I may have put my foot in it, even though I'm not sure how.' It was an effort to behave naturally when he stopped beside her and laid his hand lightly on the handle of the wheelchair.

'That sounds ominous,' he replied, glancing along the corridor. 'I saw Sandra Sullivan scurrying away so do I take it that you said something to upset her?'

'That's right.' She quickly related what the other woman had told her and saw him frown.

'I can't see how you said anything wrong, although I'm surprised to hear that she has a husband.' He glanced round as the sound of voices heralded the arrival of some early afternoon visitors. 'We can't discuss this here in the corridor. Let's go back inside.'

He pushed her wheelchair back into the day room and closed the door. The room was empty now that everyone had returned to the ward to await their visitors. Morgan switched off the television then sat down opposite her.

'Tell me exactly what Sandra told you,' he instructed.

Katrina faithfully repeated every word of their conversation then sighed. 'I've no idea why she got so upset. All I did was suggest that the police might be able to contact her husband if she asked them. She seemed terrified that he would be angry when he found out that she'd had an accident.'

'Really?' He frowned thoughtfully, deep creases appearing between his brows as he thought about what she had told him.

Katrina looked away because she was afraid that her expression might be too revealing. How many times in the past had she teased him about developing lines if he frowned like that? And how many times had she followed up her teasing by kissing the lines away? It was an effort to focus on what he was saying as the memories came rushing back.

Convinced that she hadn't heard him correctly, she repeated his words doubtfully. 'Sandra refused to give a contact name and phone number?'

'That's right.' He shrugged but his eyes were puzzled. 'Normally, I wouldn't get involved with something like that, but she was so het up when she was taken to the recovery room that the staff there asked me to have a word with her.

'I asked Theatre sister if she would get in touch with a relative in the hope that it would help to calm Sandra down if she had a member of her family with her. However, it turned out that Sandra had claimed that she didn't have any family when she was admitted. Bearing in mind what she has just told you about her husband, I can't understand why she lied.'

'Neither can I. And why on earth didn't she want her husband to know what had happened? Surely she isn't worried because she damaged the car?' It was hard to hide her incredulity and she saw him smile.

'Some people attach far more importance to material possessions than you do, Katrina.'

'I suppose they do,' she conceded. 'I just can't see any

point in worrying about *things*. It's people who matter, not
what they own.'

'A lot of people wouldn't agree with you, unfortunately.
Maybe Sandra's husband is the sort who flies off the handle
if there's the tiniest scratch on the paintwork. I've known
a few folk like that in my time,' he observed wryly.

'Thank heavens you aren't like that! I certainly wouldn't
have fallen...' She stopped, horrified by what she'd been
about to say, that she wouldn't have fallen in love with him
if he'd been so concerned about trivialities.

There was a rather awkward silence before Morgan
cleared his throat. 'Anyway, don't you go worrying about
Sandra's problems. I'll have a word with her and see if I
can sort this out. What I came to tell you was that I won't
be able to visit you tonight. I've been invited to a fund-
raising dinner in Manchester and, seeing I'm the guest of
honour, there's no way that I can get out of it.'

'It's fine. Don't worry about it,' she said quickly, hoping
that he couldn't hear the strain in her voice. It was the kind
of unconscious slip that anyone could have made.
Nevertheless, the thought of all the reasons *why* she had
fallen in love with him couldn't be dismissed so easily.

It hadn't been just the physical attraction she'd felt for
him, although that had been a very important part of it.
There had been so many things that she'd liked and admired about him. She doubted if he had changed all that
much in the intervening years, which naturally made her
wonder if it could happen all over again. Could she fall in
love with Morgan now as deeply and as completely as she
had done once before?

'I've asked Mrs Mackenzie to bring Tomàs in to see
you.' He shrugged when she looked blankly at him. 'He
looks forward to seeing you so much that it didn't seem
fair that he should miss out just because I have made other
arrangements.'

'That was kind of you,' she murmured, her heart ham-

mering as she tried to deal with the thought. 'And good of
Mrs Mackenzie to agree to help.'

'Mrs Mackenzie has been marvellous. I don't know what
I would have done without her help,' he said sincerely.
'She's staying overnight again to care for Tomàs in case
I'm back late.'

'You seem to have coped remarkably well.' She took a
deep breath then deliberately consigned the idea to the fur-
thest reaches of her mind where it could do no damage.
Falling in love with Morgan again wasn't an option!

'Only because Tomàs is such an easygoing child. He's
a real joy to be with,' he replied immediately.

She felt a ripple of pleasure race through her when she
heard the warmth in his voice. 'He seems very fond of you,
Morgan. It's obvious that the two of you have formed a
bond even in such a short time.'

'Tomàs doesn't seem to have any problem relating to
strangers,' he said flatly. 'He gets on equally well with Mrs
Mackenzie.'

She lowered her eyes because she didn't want him to see
the disappointment in them. Morgan had been warning her
not to read too much into his relationship with the child
because it wasn't going to affect his decision about the
adoption. Had she been nurturing a secret hope that he
would reconsider once he'd got to know the little boy better?

It was a relief when the door opened and Beatrice appeared because it spared her from having to answer that
question. Frankly, she'd had enough emotional turmoil for
one day and couldn't wait to make her escape. She saw
Beatrice hesitate when she spotted Morgan and quickly
wheeled herself to the door.

'Have you come to fetch me?'

'I can come back later if you like,' Beatrice offered,
glancing at Morgan for guidance.

'There's no need,' she quickly assured her. 'Dr Grey was just leaving.'

She didn't look at Morgan again as Beatrice wheeled her into the corridor. She could feel him watching her but she didn't glance round. She had to take a leaf out of his book and learn to deal with this situation as objectively as possible. If Morgan wasn't going to help her with the adoption then she would have to rethink her plans.

Beatrice got her settled then drew the curtains around the bed. There were still a few visitors in the ward so she was glad of the privacy. She switched on the radio and tried listening to some music but her mind was racing. And with every twist and turn her thoughts always arrived back at the same point. Morgan.

He had been part of her life for so long now that it wasn't going to be easy to make the final break. Even though she had accepted that their marriage was over, she hadn't *really* accepted that he would never be a part of her future. Now she had to face that fact and deal with it as sensibly as he'd done.

She frowned. Morgan seemed to have adapted to the idea far better than she had done, but why was that? How had he been able to cut her out of his life so completely and, apparently, with such little difficulty? It made her wonder all of a sudden if he had loved her as much as she had loved him.

She reached over and turned up the volume on the radio, letting the music drown out her thoughts. She didn't think she could bear it if she found out that the answer to that question was no.

The dinner had dragged on far longer than Morgan had expected it to so that it was almost midnight before he arrived back in Dalverston. He hoped that he'd managed to hide his impatience as the speeches had run on and on. Everyone else had appeared to be having a wonderful time

which had made his own eagerness to leave all the more
difficult to understand. Why *had* he been counting the
minutes until he could make his escape?

Because he'd missed Katrina.

The thought slid into his head with such speed that it
took him completely by surprise. Try as he may, he
couldn't rationalise it away. He *had* missed Katrina, had
missed spending time with her and Tomàs that evening. He
didn't want to face the truth but there was no way to avoid
it: Katrina was becoming an important part of his life again.

He was so stunned by the idea that he didn't realise at
first that he had turned into the hospital's car park instead
of carrying on through the town. He drew up close to the
main building and switched off the engine. He knew that
he wouldn't be able to sleep if he went home and the
thought of lying in bed, endlessly churning over the problem of what he should do, was more than he could bear.
What he needed was something to distract him and the one
thing guaranteed to do that was work.

He locked the car then made his way to the side entrance
which was used at night when the main doors were locked.
He keyed in the security code then opened the door when
the buzzer sounded. There were few people about as he
made his way to the lift and those he did encounter merely
nodded to him. If anyone thought it strange to see him
turning up at that hour of the night dressed in a dinner
jacket, they certainly didn't remark on it.

One of the advantages of having a reputation for being
stand-offish, he thought wryly. People tended to keep their
thoughts to themselves rather than risk a rebuff. However,
the downside was feeling that he was always the outsider,
the one standing on the fringes of the crowd. It was a feeling he'd had for most of his life, apart from the time he'd
spent with Katrina. He'd never felt more loved and wanted
than he had then.

The reminder was so bitterly painful that he drove it from

his head. The lift had arrived so he stepped inside, meaning to go straight to his office and finish the report he'd been writing earlier that day. However, just as he was about to press the button for the fifth floor he suddenly remembered that he needed some statistics from the surgical ward. Sister Carter had promised to let him have them that afternoon but, after he'd spoken to Katrina, he'd forgotten to get them off her. It would be a waste of time trying to complete the report without them.

It was very quiet when he reached the surgical ward. At that time of the night all the patients were fast asleep and the staff would be catching up on paperwork. He made his way to the office then paused when he heard voices coming from the kitchen. One of them he immediately recognised as belonging to Evelyn Leonard, the sister on duty that night, so he veered off to speak to her. It was only as he was opening the door that he heard a second voice and realised that it was Katrina's.

'There is nothing like a cup of tea when you can't sleep—' she was saying, then stopped when she saw him.

Morgan saw a wash of colour run up her face and something inside him responded instantly to the betraying sign. Katrina was as aware of him as he was of her and even though the rational side of him knew that it was a highly dangerous situation, another side rejoiced.

'Dr Grey! What are you doing here?' Evelyn Leonard exclaimed, sounding flustered at being caught unawares.

'I needed some statistics that Sister Carter kindly agreed to compile for me,' he explained, trying his best to pretend there was nothing wrong. It wasn't easy because he was deeply aware of Katrina sitting a few feet away from him.

She was wearing the same towelling robe that she'd had on the other morning, her honey-brown hair fastened up into a girlish ponytail that exposed the delicate curve of her ears and the fragile nape of her neck. Morgan found himself thinking helplessly how utterly adorable and sexy she looked, certainly not the wisest of thoughts in the circumstances.

He forced his thoughts back into line and summoned a
distinctly strained smile. 'I know it's late but is there any
chance that you could find them for me, Sister? I need them
to finish a report that I'm writing.'

'Of course.' Evelyn hurried to the door then paused and
looked back with an understanding smile. 'I'll be in the
office, Dr Grey. I'll have the figures for you whenever
you're ready.'

He cleared his throat as the woman discreetly closed the
door behind her. It was obvious to him that Sister Leonard
believed that the statistics had been merely a trumped-up
excuse for his late-night visit!

He glanced at Katrina but she had her nose buried in her
cup of tea, making it impossible to tell if she shared
Evelyn's suspicions. However, the thought that she might
imagine that he had come to the ward specifically to see
her was more than he could bear.

'Before you start reading anything into this, I assure you
that me being here has nothing whatsoever to do with you,'
he said bluntly. 'I needed those figures.'

'I'm sure you did.' She set her cup down with a thump
and glared at him. 'Don't worry, Morgan, I'm not foolish
enough to imagine that you were pining for my company.
It's the last thing I'd think, believe me!'

'What do you mean by that?' he shot back, stung into
asking a question he knew he would regret.

'Nothing! It doesn't matter.'

She went to get up then stopped when she realised that
she couldn't manage to stand by herself. His brows rose as
he saw her hit the table with her clenched fist in a fit of
pique. It was obvious that something had upset her but he
had no idea what it could be. Surely his unscheduled arrival
couldn't have prompted a reaction like this?

'What's wrong, Katrina?' He held up his hand when she

went to speak. 'No. There's no point lying because I know you too well. I can tell when something has upset you.'

'Bully for you! Aren't you the clever one?' she taunted, but he could hear the misery in her voice and see the anguish that had clouded her hazel eyes.

'Not really,' he replied in a tone that was far more gentle than he had intended it to be. However, there was no way that he could harden his heart. Katrina was hurt and upset, and if there was anything he could do to help her then nothing on earth would stop him.

He crouched in front of her so that she was forced to look at him, feeling his heart twist when he saw her bite hard on her lower lip to stop it trembling. 'I just know that there's something wrong and I want you to tell me what it is.'

He looked deep into her eyes, willing her to trust him, wondering if she could after what had happened between them. All of a sudden that thought was almost too painful to bear. He wasn't sure he could cope with knowing that Katrina no longer trusted him...

'Did you ever really love me, Morgan?'

His heart seemed to come to a dead stop when he realised what she'd said. All he could do was stare at her because he was having such difficulty assimilating the question. Why on earth had she asked him a question like that? he wondered incredulously. Surely she must know the answer? Unless...unless she was trying to tell him something?

'What exactly are you getting at, Katrina?'

He stood up abruptly and went to the sink, then stood with his back to her. There was a sick feeling in the pit of his stomach, an ache in his gut that made him want to double up in agony, only years of self-discipline meant that he had to conceal his pain.

'It was a simple enough question but maybe I already know the answer,' she shot back. 'Forget it, Morgan. It doesn't matter.'

'Of course it matters!' He swung round to face her, wondering if she had any idea how he was feeling at that moment. Did she know that she had the power to destroy everything that he'd held precious with a few simple words? But no matter how painful this was, he had to know what she was trying to tell him.

'You asked me if I had ever really loved you, but maybe what you were trying to say was that you never really loved me.' He saw the colour drain from her face, but made himself remain where he was because he simply didn't have enough sympathy to spare for her when he needed every scrap of it himself.

'Was that what it was leading up to, Katrina? Were you hoping that we could swop confidences and tell the truth at last? Well, don't stop now. Let's get this sorted out once and for all. Did you love me, Katrina, or have you realised that you were mistaken about your feelings?'

CHAPTER SEVEN

KATRINA could feel her heart pounding so hard that it was making her feel sick. The expression on Morgan's face was frankly scary but it wasn't that which frightened her most. She had never meant that question to slip out, and never dreamed that he would turn the tables on her the way he had! Now she wasn't sure what to say. If she admitted that she had been head over heels in love with him, would it make the present situation better or worse?

He smiled thinly when she didn't answer. 'It isn't like you to prevaricate, Katrina. Normally you're completely honest except if you're worried about hurting someone's feelings. If that's the case now then I assure you that I won't go to pieces. I'm past that stage now.'

She felt a little flare of resentment heat her blood when she heard the taunting note in his voice. 'I'm sure you are, which makes it difficult for me to understand why you're interested in how I felt four years ago. I mean, that's all in the past, isn't it, Morgan? It doesn't have any bearing on the current situation.'

'I agree, but it was you who started this. Remember?' His smile was tinged with ice, his green eyes so chilly that she shivered. 'You were the one who asked me if I'd ever *really* loved you, if you recall.'

She hated to hear him taunting her that way but she'd be damned if she'd let him see how much it had hurt. 'Mmm, silly of me, wasn't it?'

Katrina managed a light laugh, rather pleased by the fact that it had sounded so insouciant. 'In another couple of weeks I'll be out of your hair for good so there doesn't seem much point rehashing our past relationship. Put it down to a lack of sleep and incipient boredom. It gives the mind far too much time to dwell on trivialities, I'm afraid. Sorry!'

He inclined his head. 'Apology accepted. We'll leave it at that.' He shot his cuff up and checked his watch. 'It's later than I thought. Maybe it would be better if I went home and left that report until another day. I'm probably too tired to concentrate, if the truth be known.'

She smiled gamely, refusing to let him guess the depth of her despair. He might not have answered her question but did she need him to? Hadn't he made his position perfectly clear?

There was an ache in her heart that felt so very real that instinctively she pressed her hand to her chest to ease it. She saw him frown when he noticed what she had done.

'Are you all right?' he demanded, quickly moving back to the table.

'Fine.' She shook her head when it appeared that he was going to say something else. 'Don't fuss, Morgan! I'm perfectly fine, or I will be just as soon as I get out of this damned place!'

'It will be a couple of weeks before you'll be fit enough to be discharged,' he said flatly. 'And even then you won't be able to do very much for yourself.'

'I know that.' She refused to look at him, not sure that she could bear to see the aloof expression that was bound to be on his face. Morgan had slipped back into the role of doctor once again, and whilst part of her knew that it was best this way the other, foolish part hated to have him treat her so distantly.

'Do you? I'm not convinced that you realise just how difficult your life is going to be for the next few months,' he stated bluntly. 'You're going to need help to look after yourself let alone take care of Tomàs. Have you given any thought to what you're going to do?'

'Not yet but, as I said, I have a lot of time on my hands at the present. I'm sure I can work something out.'

She smiled sweetly up at him, refusing to let him guess how worried she was about coping on her own in the coming months. 'Don't worry, Morgan. I don't expect you to come to my rescue. So if it's that which has been giving you sleepless nights of late then put it right out of your mind. Your involvement ends the minute I leave here.'

'So long as you understand the situation that's fine.' His tone was curt. 'I'll see you tomorrow afternoon when I bring Tomàs in to visit you. Goodnight.'

'Morgan, I...'

She stopped when she realised that she was talking to fresh air. She picked up the cup but her hands were trembling too hard to hold it steady. She put it down on the table again, desperately wishing that she could go back to the beginning and replay that scene all over again. If she could do that, she wouldn't say half the things she'd said...

Katrina sighed. *If.* It was such a little word yet such a powerful one. It had been the word which had haunted her for the past four years.

If she'd never told Morgan how much she'd wanted a family then he wouldn't have felt so bad about not being able to father a child.

If she'd been able to convince him that they could be happy without children then they might still be together.

If they hadn't parted then she would never have met Rosa and Tomàs.

She smiled wistfully. *If* could precede good things as well as bad. She had to remember that. *If* could mark the beginning, not just the end.

The ward was a hive of activity on Saturday morning. A lot of patients were being discharged that day so there was much coming and going as people packed up their belongings ready to return to their homes. Katrina couldn't help feeling rather envious but at least she had the previously cancelled physiotherapy session to look forward to, and that should help to relieve some of the monotony. There was a new staff nurse on duty that day and she volunteered to take Katrina to the physio unit as all the porters were busy. She introduced herself on the way to the lift.

'I'm Maggie Carr, by the way. It was my fiancé, Luke Fabrizzi, who operated on you.'

Katrina smiled at the other woman with genuine pleasure. 'It's lovely to meet you! Luke has told me such a lot about you.' She frowned. 'I thought you were working on the children's ward, though?'

'I was,' Maggie replied cheerfully, whizzing her into the lift and pressing the button for the ground floor, where the physiotherapy unit was situated. 'Still am, in fact. I'm just filling in for the weekend because Surgical was short-staffed.'

She leant against the wall and grinned at Katrina. 'I used to be on the surgical ward but the powers that be obviously thought that I wouldn't be able to keep my mind on the job if I had to work with Luke so I was moved. They could have been right, too!'

'Not that you'd tell them that!' She laughed when Maggie rolled her eyes. 'Mmm, little changes, I see. I remember there being a bit of a to-do once it was discovered that Morgan and I were an item.'

'So you two worked together at one time, did you?' Maggie asked curiously, pushing the chair out of the lift as the doors opened. 'I asked Luke but you know how useless men are—they *never* find out the important details!'

'I do.' Katrina smiled. 'Morgan was always hopeless when it came to any gossip. Mind you, I don't suppose he ever imagined that he would be taking centre stage.'

'You mean all the talk that's been flying around since you turned up out of the blue?' Maggie didn't pretend not to understand and Katrina was grateful for that. It made her

Play The *Lucky Hearts* Game

and get... FREE BOOKS & a FREE GIFT... YOURS to KEEP!

Yes! I have scratched off the silver card. Please send me my **FREE BOOKS** and **FREE MYSTERY GIFT**. I understand that I am under no obligation to purchase any books as explained on the back of this card. I am over 18 years of age.

Scratch Here! then look below to see what you can claim...

M2BI

Mrs/Miss/Ms/Mr   Initials

BLOCK CAPITALS PLEASE

Surname

Address

Postcode

Twenty-one gets you
2 FREE BOOKS and a
MYSTERY GIFT!

Twenty gets you
1 FREE BOOK and a
MYSTERY GIFT!

Nineteen gets you
1 FREE BOOK!

TRY AGAIN!

The Reader Service™ — Here's how it works:

Accepting your free books places you under no obligation to buy anything. You may keep the books and gift and return the despatch note marked "cancel." If we do not hear from you, about a month later we'll send you 4 brand new books and invoice you just £2.49* each. That's the complete price — there is no extra charge for postage and packing. You may cancel at any time, otherwise every month we'll send you 4 more books, which you may either purchase or return to us — the choice is yours.

*Terms and prices subject to change without notice.

NO STAMP NEEDED!

THE READER SERVICE™
FREE BOOK OFFER
FREEPOST CN81
CROYDON
CR9 3WZ

NO STAMP
NECESSARY
IF POSTED IN
THE U.K. OR N.I.

even more certain that she could trust the other woman. She had taken an immediate liking to Maggie Carr and didn't feel at all worried that Maggie would repeat what she said.

'Yes. From what I can gather, nobody knew that Morgan was married until I was admitted.'

'That's right. He never mentioned you, which was why it was such a surprise. Mind you, I don't know why it should have been. It's not as if he ever talks about his personal life.'

Maggie swung round and used her backside to open the swing doors to the physio unit. She paused once they were safely inside and looked at Katrina. 'Tell me to mind my own business if you like, but if you ever need a friendly ear, mine is available. I'm not sure what's going on and I don't want you to think that I'm prying, but if I can help in any way...' She shrugged expressively.

'Thanks. I appreciate that, Maggie.' She sighed. 'However, I think everything is sorted out even if it hasn't gone as I had hoped it would. I wanted Morgan to help me legalise Tomàs's adoption with the British courts,' she explained. 'He refused. End of story.'

'I see. A bit of a blow, I imagine. But are you sure that there's no way that you can persuade him to change his mind? Luke has told me how fond Morgan is of the little boy. He never stops talking about him, apparently.'

'Doesn't he?' Katrina smiled wistfully. 'That's nice to hear, but once Morgan makes up his mind he can be—'

'As stubborn as a mule,' Maggie finished for her. 'I know because Luke is exactly the same! Anyway, the offer's there if you ever want to take me up on it. Right, time for your torture now. Thumb screws and boiling oil, all in the name of restoring you to full health and vitality!'

Katrina laughed as Maggie briskly wheeled her into the physio's room. The cloud that had been hanging over seemed to have lifted a little, thanks to the other woman's kindness. The confrontation she'd had with Morgan had weighed on her mind all night long, but she had to put it behind her, although she couldn't help wondering if Maggie had been right about not giving up. Maybe she could persuade him, and if she could then...

She groaned.

No more ifs!

Tomàs was an early riser so Morgan was up by six and in the park by seven. He'd happened to notice the playground as he'd been driving home the previous night and, as the little boy was so full of energy, had decided that it would be the perfect place to let him run off some steam.

He followed as Tomàs raced from the slide to the swings then on to the see-saw, marvelling at his energy. Frankly, he himself felt as though he'd been left out in the rain too long—all sort of grey and washed out, as though there were no colour left inside him. The memory of what Katrina had said the previous night seemed to have erased what tiny bit of happiness that had been left in his heart.

She hadn't really loved him. For all these years he'd been living under an erroneous assumption, and it hurt to know that. It hurt a lot.

'Papa! Look.'

Morgan blinked and everything shot back into focus. He felt his heart turn over when he saw Tomàs dangling precariously from the top of the climbing frame. He had already started running when the little boy suddenly let out a shrill scream as he lost his grip and landed with a thud on the rubber mat.

'Are you all right? Where does it hurt?' he demanded as he dropped to his knees beside the child. He ran his hand over the little boy's head, feeling panic setting in when he felt the lump on the back of Tomàs's skull. Just for a second every scrap of medical knowledge seemed to disappear from his mind so that he wasn't sure what to do.

Should he pick up Tomàs and carry him home? Or should he leave him there and call for an ambulance? It was only when the little boy let out a loud wail that his brain mercifully cleared.

'Lie still,' he instructed, quickly checking the child's limbs for any signs of fractures. From what he could tell, there was no real damage apart from the bump on his head, and that would need to be checked out in hospital. Hopefully, it would turn out to be nothing more than a lump but he wouldn't take any risks. Katrina would never forgive him if he let anything happen to the child.

His mind took a small step sideways. *He* would never forgive himself, never mind Katrina!

Morgan carried Tomàs back to the car and his hands were perfectly steady as he strapped him in, which was surprising. To realise how much the child meant to him had been a shock after all. He should be going through agonies, wondering how to deal with it or, rather, how to find a way to ignore it. Wasn't that how he'd always dealt with difficult emotional issues in the past? Even deciding that his marriage had to end had been partly a means of avoidance. He hadn't felt able to deal with Katrina's pain about not having children so he'd decided that it would be better if they split up.

It was as though a light had gone on and he was suddenly unable to hide from the truth any longer: He was an emotional cripple because of the way he had been brought up. Admitting it was the first step, doing something about it was the second, but all of a sudden he was afraid that he wouldn't have the courage to confront the demons from his past and vanquish them.

He got into the car then turned to look at the little boy. Despite the fright he'd had, Tomàs treated him to a beaming smile. Morgan's heart turned over again. If he could find the courage to take that difficult second step then his whole life might change.

* * *

'He's fine. Obviously, you'll need to keep an eye on him for the next twenty-four hours, but there's really no need to worry. The scan was clear.'

Morgan sighed in relief as the young houseman gave him the good news. He thanked the younger doctor then went back to the cubicle, where Tomàs was waiting for him. The child had been as good as gold while he'd had the CT scan. He'd seemed more fascinated by the high-tech equipment than afraid. Now, as he lifted the little boy off the bed and took hold of his hand, Morgan felt a deep sense of relief and pride. There couldn't be many children of this age who would have coped so well.

'You were really brave, Tomàs. *Muy…*' He struggled for the word he wanted as Tomàs stared trustingly up at him.

'*Valeroso.*'

A familiar voice had supplied the word he'd been searching for. Morgan felt a ripple of pure guilt run through him when he looked up and saw Katrina watching them. It was blatantly obvious that she wasn't pleased, not that he could blame her.

'*Muy valeroso.* I think that's what you were trying to say, wasn't it, Morgan?' She smiled frostily at him. 'What I'd like to know now is what Tomàs is doing in the A and E unit?'

'I…um…' A wash of colour raced up his face when he heard the cutting note in her voice. He was just trying to find a tactful way to explain what had happened when Tomàs decided to fill in the missing details.

Katrina's expression grew colder than ever as the child related his adventures. Sliding her arm protectively around the little boy's shoulders, she treated Morgan to a look that could have drawn blood.

'Is it that hard to keep an eye on a three-year-old? Really, Morgan, I would have thought you'd have had more sense. Tomàs should *never* have been allowed to go on that climbing frame in the first place!'

Morgan took a deep breath. Quite apart from the fact that he was very much aware that the staff in the A and E unit were following what was going on with interest, it would be wrong to snap at her when she had every right to be angry.

'You're quite right and I assure you that it won't happen again,' he said tersely.

He took hold of her wheelchair and swiftly pushed her out of the waiting room, not stopping until they reached a quiet alcove well away from the hustle and bustle. It was used during the week by patients for the gastroenterology department, but the department wasn't open on a Saturday. There was a drinks machine against one wall so he bought Tomàs a carton of fruit juice and got him settled on a chair with a comic then went back to her.

'It was an accident, Katrina. I know it should never have happened and believe me, I feel really bad about it. However, the good news is that Tomàs has had a CAT scan and there's no sign of any damage.' He sighed when she continued to stare coldly up at him. 'He's got a lump on the back of his head but he's fine. Really. I promise.'

'Good.' Her tone was clipped but that didn't mean he couldn't hear the fear it held as well. He was beset by remorse as he crouched in front of her and took hold of her hands.

'It must have given you a real scare when you found out what had happened and I'm sorry.' He frowned as a thought struck him. 'How did you find out, though?'

'We met one of the nurses from A and E on the way back from the physio unit and she told me that you'd brought Tomàs in.' She took a deep breath and he saw a little colour return to her face. 'Maggie took me straight there so that I could make sure that he was all right.'

'Maggie?' he repeated vaguely before his brain made the connection. 'Oh, Luke's Maggie, you mean. Luke said that she was filling in on Surgical this weekend.' He looked round uncertainly. 'Where is she now?'

'She had to get back to the ward,' Katrina explained. 'She said that I could get one of the A and E staff to phone her when I was ready to go back. We weren't sure how long you'd be in the radiology unit, you see.'

'Thankfully, there wasn't a queue for once, so it was all over and done with in record time. And, as I said, Tomàs is fine, not that it absolves me, of course. I should never have let him fall in the first place,' he admitted frankly.

'It wasn't your fault, I don't imagine.' She returned the gentle pressure of his fingers and smiled. 'Tomàs is a real little daredevil. He has no sense of fear, I'm afraid!'

'Thanks for the warning!' he declared wryly, although it was hard to ignore the way his heart was racing all of a sudden. When Katrina smiled at him like that, it made him feel ten feet tall and as though he could move mountains!

So how about moving a few now? a small voice inside whispered. How about taking that second step along the road to redemption? Was he big enough and brave enough to tell her about his past and how it had influenced him?

'Morgan, what is it? Is something wrong?'

He sighed when he heard the concern in her voice because he hadn't realised that his expression had been so revealing. He longed to tell her the truth but the problem was that it was neither the time nor the place for an in-depth conversation, although that might be simply an excuse to avoid it. Hadn't he dreamt up any number of similar excuses over the years?

'Nothing.' He pushed that last thought to the back of his mind because it wasn't easy to admit that he was such a coward when it came to his personal life.

'Nothing?' she mocked. 'So that's why you were looking as though you had the weight of the world on your shoulders, was it?'

'I was just thinking about what happened this morning,' he hedged. He glanced at Tomàs and burst out laughing. 'Doesn't look as though there's much wrong with him now, does there?'

'There certainly doesn't.' Katrina laughed as well as she watched the little boy pushing the empty juice carton across the floor. 'What do you think he's pretending it is, a car or a boat?'

'I'm not sure. The trouble is that you forget how to play when you're grown up, don't you?' he observed rather wistfully.

'You do. If only we could see the world through the eyes of a child then most problems would appear far less complicated.' She shrugged when he looked at her. 'If you or I were trying to construct a car or a boat, we'd get so caught up by the trivialities that we'd miss out on the fun. I mean, a drink carton doesn't really resemble either, does it? It's got no wheels or sails...'

'Or bumpers or horns,' Morgan put in, chuckling. 'Oh, the joys of living in such an uncomplicated world. Children are so lucky, aren't they?'

'Some of them are. Others aren't so fortunate.'

She took a deep breath but there was a note in her voice all of a sudden that made his pulse race. 'I want Tomàs to be one of the lucky ones. Maybe it's selfish, but I want to give him everything he needs to make his childhood special. I don't mean material things because they don't matter nearly as much as knowing that he's loved and wanted, that there will always be someone to turn to if he needs help.'

She looked him straight in the eye and he could almost *feel* the force of emotion that was issuing from her. 'That's one of the reasons why I wanted you to help me with his adoption, Morgan. If anything happened to me, I wanted to know that Tomàs could turn to you for guidance. I know that I can trust you always to do your very best once you've made a promise.'

He was so moved that he couldn't speak. All he could do was squeeze her hands, hoping that she would understand everything that he couldn't put into words. Katrina was prepared to trust him with the most precious thing in her life and he couldn't describe how that made him feel.

She suddenly reached up and her fingers felt so cool as they brushed his cheek. 'Don't torture yourself. I didn't tell you that so it would cause you pain. I do understand, you know.'

'Do you?' His voice was husky, aching with a need to let her know how moved he was.

'Yes. You don't want to get involved and I'm not trying to make you feel bad about it—' she began, only he didn't let her finish, couldn't let another misunderstanding arise. He'd made that mistake last night by not telling her how much he had loved her. Maybe it wouldn't have made any difference to how she had felt about him, but it would have felt so much better to know that he'd been honest with her, brave and not a coward!

'I don't feel bad about my decision.' He paused, realising that wasn't quite true. However, he wasn't sure that he knew how to phrase it any better so carried on, 'I was touched by the fact that you would trust me to take care of Tomàs for you. It means an awful lot to me, Katrina, and I want you to know that.'

He took a deep breath and hurried on before his courage deserted him once more. 'I also want to clarify something you asked me last night.'

'It doesn't matter now,' she said quickly, trying to withdraw her hand.

'It does.' He held onto it, refusing to let her go until he'd said what needed to be said. 'You asked me if I had ever really loved you. Well, the answer is yes. I loved you with my whole heart, Katrina. There should never be any doubt about that.'

He saw her eyes brim with tears. 'Oh, Morgan, I'm such an idiot! I thought you were trying to tell me that...'

'No!' He sighed. 'But I don't want you to get upset because you weren't really in love with me.'

'Hold on a moment, I never said that!' she declared forcefully.

'But I thought—'

'Then you thought wrong!' she shot back, before her voice softened. 'I was madly in love with you, Morgan, from the minute I met you.'

He felt as though he were suddenly floating on air as a feeling of euphoria filled him. Katrina *had* loved him! He *hadn't* been mistaken! He *could* still cling to his precious memories of their time together!

'Thank you. It means such a lot to hear you say that,' he confessed. He leant forward to kiss her cheek, afraid of what might be written on his face at that moment. It felt as though his heart were filled with music all of a sudden, as though his life were once again painted in colour rather than in shades of grey. Katrina had loved him. Nothing could detract from that simple, glorious fact.

'I'm glad,' she began, looking up at the same moment as he bent towards her. Whatever else she'd been going to say didn't get uttered as their mouths touched.

Morgan's heart took a great, bounding leap when he felt the softness of her lips beneath his. The contact might have been purely accidental but his reaction to it had been pre-ordained. Every cell in his body suddenly went on alert as it received the signals. Katrina's here. Prepare!

'Oh, hell!' The oath was swallowed up as he leant forward that bit more so that his lips could settle more firmly over hers. There was nothing accidental about *this* kiss, he realised giddily as his mouth took immediate charge. This was wholly premeditated, planned and honed to perfection during four very long years.

Katrina moaned softly as he gently drew her lower lip

into his mouth. Morgan's blood pressure zipped several notches up the scale when he heard the betraying little sound. Emboldened, he let the tip of his tongue skate delicately, provocatively, across the moist inner curve of her upper lip, and heard her sigh. Up went his blood pressure that bit more.

He pulled her into his arms at that point, unable to resist. It was awkward because of the wheelchair and he couldn't stifle his groan when he felt her knee pressing into his groin. A wave of heat enveloped him as his body responded with unnerving speed to the pressure. He could tell at once that Katrina had felt what had happened, but he wasn't embarrassed. Why should he be embarrassed when her response was every bit as blatant as his?

His whole body felt as though it were suddenly on fire when he felt her nipples harden. He could feel them eagerly pressing into his chest so that the softness of her breasts seemed all the more marked in contrast. He wanted to cup her breasts in his hands, stroke them, caress them and enjoy them as he had done so many times in the past. He might even have been tempted to do so if the part of his mind that was still able to function rationally hadn't warned him that this wasn't the place to indulge in such delights. He had to content himself with a kiss for now and save everything else until another time...

The thought jarred. There wouldn't be another time, though. There couldn't be. Their marriage was over. Never again would he and Katrina be lovers.

Katrina's beautiful face was flushed with passion when he drew back. Morgan felt a dagger of red-hot pain spear through his heart when she opened her eyes and looked at him with such trust. He prayed that he wasn't going to disappoint her again, yet feared that he would the moment she spoke.

'Where do we go from here, Morgan?'

He took a deep breath.

Where indeed?

CHAPTER EIGHT

'IT WOULD be wrong to read too much into what just happened, Katrina.'

Katrina felt her heart flutter when she heard the grating note in Morgan's voice. It was hard to feign a composure she didn't feel, but she refused to let him see how nervous she felt all of a sudden. That kiss had taken her completely by surprise for a number of reasons.

She had never expected him to lower his defences like that, neither had she imagined that she would be so susceptible when he did. It was bound to have repercussions and there was no way that either of them could deny that.

'Would it?' she said blandly, although her heart was racing.

'Of course!' He ran his hand through his hair and there was more than a hint of impatience to the gesture. 'These things happen all the time, Katrina...'

'Maybe they happen to you but they don't happen to me.' She took a deep breath but there was no way that she would lie simply because it was easier. 'You wanted me just now, Morgan, just as I wanted you. Maybe you would have felt exactly the same with another woman in similar circumstances and I'm certainly not in any position to dispute that. However, I assure you that I don't usually go around kissing men the way I just kissed you!'

He bit out a low oath. 'What do you want me to say, Katrina? That you're right? That I *did* want you? That, no, it wouldn't have been the same with another woman? All right, then, yes to all of those. However, it doesn't have any bearing on the current situation.'

'In other words, the fact that we enjoy kissing each other

107

doesn't mean that we are going to get back together?' She gave a brittle laugh, wondering if she really *had* been foolish enough to wish that could happen. It had been a kind of madness. When he'd held her in his arms, all she'd been able to think about had been how right it had felt.

'Yes! We can't go back, Katrina. It's impossible. Nothing has changed.' He stood in front of her, big and arrogant as he tried to dictate the terms. Katrina felt her temper rise with a speed that would have shocked her if she hadn't been too hurt to feel shocked.

'Who said that I wanted to go back? Don't flatter yourself, Morgan. Never heard the saying, "Once bitten, twice shy"?'

'Yes, I've heard it and taken heed of it, just as you obviously have. At least we both know where we stand.' His tone was clipped, his face expressionless, so how did she know that she had hurt him deeply?

She half reached towards him then let her hand fall back to her lap when he turned away. What could she have said to him, anyway? That she was sorry? Would that really have made any difference at this point?

'I'd better get you back to the ward before they send out a search party.' He called to Tomàs then took hold of her wheelchair and turned it around.

She took a steadying breath. Hurting Morgan was the last thing she had wanted to do, yet she seemed to do nothing else at every turn. It was an effort to respond in the same deliberately light vein. 'They might think that I've taken the opportunity to make my escape.'

'You make it sound more like a prison than a hospital.' He wheeled her swiftly along the corridor to the lift. 'I don't know what we're doing wrong to make our patients so eager to leave us.'

She laughed shakily, appreciating his efforts to ease the tension. 'I'm not *quite* as keen as Sandra Sullivan is, although I must confess that I find it rather frustrating, being here.'

'I expect you do.' The lift arrived and he made sure that Tomàs was safely on board before wheeling her inside. 'It's hard to do nothing all day, although you're going to have to get used to that, I'm afraid.'

'I know.' She sighed wistfully, pleased on one hand that a certain harmony had been achieved yet knowing deep down that they were merely skating over the issues rather than dealing with them. Morgan had wanted her. She had wanted him. It had to mean something, surely?

She forced that thought to the back of her mind because it was pointless worrying about it. 'It's not going to be easy coping on my own when I get back home. Apart from anything else, our flat is on the top floor and there's no lift. I shall have to practise hopping up and down the stairs, I suppose.'

'That's going to present a real problem.' He frowned heavily. 'Have you no friends or neighbours who could help you?'

'I've lost touch with the friends I had as a child, and I've not been there long enough to get to know anyone else really well, certainly not well enough to ask them to fetch and carry for me.'

'Then it seems to me that there's only one sensible solution to the problem.'

He deftly manoeuvred the chair out of the lift as they reached their floor. Tomàs went skipping on ahead and held the door open as Morgan pushed her into the ward. Katrina waited until they had stopped beside her bed before prompting him to continue, wondering why she had a funny fizzing sensation in the pit of her stomach, rather like the attacks of exam nerves she'd suffered during her training.

'What solution?'

'That you and Tomàs come to stay with me until you're

mobile again.' He shrugged. 'I can't think of a better plan. Can you?'

What was she going to do?

All afternoon long, Katrina had tried to decide but she was no closer to making up her mind by the time the night staff came on duty. There were several unfamiliar faces that night—agency nurses, or so Maggie had told her—so nobody bothered with her apart from a cursory enquiry to see if she needed anything.

She couldn't help wishing that one of the regular members of staff had been rostered to work. At least then she'd have had someone to talk to and take her mind off her problems. It was a welcome distraction, therefore, when Graham Walker, the musician who'd had an operation on his hand, approached her bed, carrying a bundle of magazines.

'I wondered if you might like to swop,' he suggested, glancing at the pile of magazines on her bedside locker. The surgical ward was a mixed one, although folding double doors separated the male and female sections. Katrina saw Graham look ruefully over his shoulder as a cheer erupted from the men's section.

'Everyone's listening to football on the radio up our end so I've spent the past hour reading. I've finished everything I had so now I'm on the lookout for something fresh otherwise I'm in serious danger of dying of boredom!'

She laughed sympathetically. 'Obviously not a football fan, I see. Anyway, I'll happily swop with you. I've read all that lot so I could do with something new for tonight. But why don't you sit down for a few minutes and have a chat?'

'Sure I'm not disturbing you?' Graham said, quickly sitting down when she shook her head. 'Thanks. I didn't fancy another hour of my own company, to be honest. They're great blokes but it's a bit difficult to join in the conversation when you're not into sport.'

'You're a cellist, I believe.' She grinned when she saw his surprise. 'Hospital grapevines are notorious, I'm afraid. You can't keep any secrets in a place like this.'

'I suppose not,' he replied cheerfully. 'Not that I've got many to keep. What you see is what you get, unfortunately!'

'Don't go putting yourself down! I wish I was musical.'

They chatted for some time while Graham told her about the places he had visited. He played with one of the north-west's leading orchestras and had travelled extensively. However, he didn't try to monopolise the conversation and seemed genuinely interested in the work she had done. Katrina really enjoyed their conversation and was sorry when he got up to leave. It had helped for a short while to take her mind off the problem of what to do about Morgan's invitation.

'I'd better go before I talk your ears off,' Graham declared. He swopped his pile of magazines for the ones on her locker then glanced round as Sandra walked past and got into bed. Katrina was surprised when she saw the troubled expression on his face as he turned back to her.

'Is something wrong?' she asked curiously.

'I'm not sure.' Graham lowered his voice but she could hear the concern it held. 'I came across Sandra in the day room earlier today and she was sobbing her heart out. I asked her if there was anything I could do to help but she gave me the brush-off.'

'Sandra has been brusque with a lot of people,' Katrina quickly explained, not wanting Graham to get upset. He seemed a rather sensitive man to her and she would hate to think that he had taken Sandra's rudeness to heart.

'Oh, I'm not worried about that,' he assured her. 'I just don't like to see anyone looking as wretched as that poor woman does. Not that I know much about women, mind.

I'm the world's worst when it comes to relationships. That's why I'm still a bachelor and likely to stay that way!'

She laughed dutifully although she couldn't help feeling worried about what he'd said. She glanced across at Sandra and was surprised when the woman gave her a tentative smile.

'Why don't you go over and have a word with her now?' she suggested impulsively. She saw Graham hesitate and hurried on. Call it instinct but something told her that Sandra might respond to Graham's gently sympathetic manner.

'I'd go myself but I'm a bit hampered by this leg and I don't like to bother the staff when they're so busy. Sandra looks so lonely, sitting there on her own with no one to talk to.'

'All right, then, you've talked me into it. She can only tell me to get lost, can't she?'

Graham squared his shoulders then went over to Sandra's bed. Katrina held her breath as she watched him say something to the woman. She smiled in relief when she saw him sit down. Maybe that was one problem on its way to being solved.

She sighed. If only she could find a solution to her own problems now. Whilst part of her knew that it would make sense to accept Morgan's invitation to stay with him, another part wasn't convinced it would be the right thing to do. Would it really be wise to get used to having him around again?

Evening visiting began a short time later and she was surprised to see that Morgan had come on his own that night. He sat down and smiled reassuringly at her.

'Don't panic. Tomàs is fine. He's completely worn out so I put him to bed early. Mrs Mackenzie is with him.'

'Poor little mite,' she exclaimed. 'Anyway, you shouldn't have bothered coming tonight. I don't expect you to keep visiting me like this.'

'I'm sorry. I didn't mean to intrude,' he began stiffly.

'You aren't! And I didn't mean it like that.' She caught hold of his hand when he started to push back his chair. 'Please, stay. I just didn't want you to feel that you *had* to visit me. I know how busy you are with work, and then there's all the added problems you've had to contend with of late, looking after Tomàs.'

'Think I'll be canonised eventually?' he asked drily. 'I must be notching up brownie points by the cartload. Maybe one day I'll get my just rewards and be hailed a saint for having endured such hardships.'

She rolled her eyes. 'There is no need to be sarcastic!'

'Me?' He affected a hurt expression that made her laugh.

'Yes, you! Don't sit there looking innocent. I know you too well, Morgan Grey, remember? I know what a wicked sense of humour you have.'

'Not many people around here would agree with you,' he countered. 'I have a reputation for being totally lacking in humour, I'm afraid.'

'Probably well deserved, too,' she said pithily. 'I know how stuffy and offputting you can be when you set your mind to it.'

'I didn't put you off when we met, did I? Mind you, I didn't try all that hard.'

He turned her hand over and studied her palm. Katrina breathed in deeply but her heart was beating far too fast all of a sudden. 'No, you didn't. Not that there would have been much point. I'd already decided that I wanted to get to know you better.'

His lips quirked into a slight smile although he didn't look at her as he traced the calluses on her palm with his thumb. Katrina had a feeling that he was deliberately avoiding looking at her and the idea sent hot and cold chills down her spine. Morgan had always been an expert at hiding his feelings in the past so why did she know that he was having difficulty doing so now?

'Where did you get these?'

'We had to draw water from a well where I was working last. It was hard work and we all ended up with calluses for our efforts.'

She forced herself not to betray how nervous she felt, but the idea had unsettled her. She couldn't help wondering why he was finding it so hard to remain detached at the moment. Was it because she had altered the equation by bringing Tomàs into his life? Or had it something to do with that kiss they had shared earlier in the day?

'You certainly didn't choose the easy option by deciding to work overseas, Katrina.'

'I enjoyed it, though. I wouldn't have missed the experience for anything.'

'It wouldn't have happened if we'd not split up,' he reminded her.

'No. It's funny how things work out, isn't it?' she agreed softly.

'It is.' He ran his thumb over the roughened skin once more then let go of her hand. 'If we hadn't split up then you wouldn't have gone to South America and wouldn't now have Tomàs.'

'Something good that came out of something bad,' she said as lightly as she could. She took a quick breath, refusing to let herself dwell on all the questions that had peppered her thoughts.

'I really do appreciate everything you've done for him, Morgan. I never intended to involve you to such an extent.'

'I know. You told me that you didn't expect anything more than my name,' he said bluntly.

'I thought it would be what you'd want.' She frowned because she'd heard the edge in his voice. 'Was I wrong?'

'Yes. I couldn't simply put my name to a bit of paper and leave it at that. It wouldn't be fair to Tomàs, for a start.'

'You could play as big or as small a role in his life as

you wanted to. There are no hard and fast rules in this situation.' She met his gaze squarely. 'It would be entirely up to you.'

'I don't think it's that simple. If I took on a bigger role in the child's life, there's no way that I could step aside at a later date. It would only confuse him.'

'Step aside?' she queried, frowning. 'Why should you do that?'

'If you decided to get married again. Obviously, that would change the status quo, and have repercussions for Tomàs.'

Katrina frowned when she heard the grating note in his voice because she wasn't sure what had caused it. Surely it wasn't the thought of her getting married again that was worrying him?

'I have no plans to remarry so that isn't a consideration right now,' she said firmly, wanting to make her position clear.

'Maybe not at the moment but it could happen at some point in the future,' he insisted.

'And that's the reason why you won't help me with the adoption?'

'It's one of the reasons, although it certainly isn't the only one, I assure you.' He paused and she had the feeling that he was trying to decide what else to say before he suddenly shrugged. 'I just know that it would be the wrong thing for me to do.'

'In other words, you aren't going to change your mind,' she said quietly, struggling to hide her disappointment because for a moment she'd hoped that he might have been having second thoughts about his decision.

'No. It would be a mistake, as I've already explained.' He suddenly pushed back his chair and stood up. 'Anyway, I'd better be off. I don't want to play upon Mrs Mackenzie's good nature too much. I'll bring Tomàs in to see you tomorrow.'

'Thank you.'

Katrina watched him leave, wondering why she felt so unsettled by the conversation. Naturally, it had been disappointing to have had her hopes raised then dashed, but it wasn't only that. She had the strangest feeling that he had been on the verge of telling her something before he'd thought better of it, and something important, too. What on earth could it have been?

She glanced up as a man walked past the end of her bed and frowned when she saw him go over to Sandra. Graham was still talking to Sandra and she saw him look round in surprise when he heard the newcomer approaching. It was obvious that Sandra hadn't been expecting the visitor because it was hard to miss the stricken expression that crossed her face as the man bent and kissed her.

Graham quickly got up, looking distinctly uncomfortable as he hurried back to his end of the ward. Another party arrived just then to visit the woman in the bed next to Katrina's. They found themselves chairs and made a circle around their friend's bed, blocking Katrina's view of what was happening across the aisle. Not that it was any of her business, really, although she couldn't help wondering if the man was Sandra's husband. But if he was, why had Sandra looked so shocked?

She sighed wearily. Why did one question always lead to another?

He had come so close to telling Katrina the truth tonight!

Morgan got up and went to the window, unable to settle. The view over the town was magnificent at night but it didn't soothe him as it usually did. All evening long he had endlessly replayed that moment when he'd almost told Katrina the truth about why he wouldn't help her to adopt Tomàs.

It had been on the tip of his tongue but at the very last second he hadn't been able to go through with it and he hated the feeling that he'd behaved like a coward. He was a grown man of nearly forty, for heaven's sake! He should be able to deal with his past. He *would* deal with it. Now. He would go back to the hospital this very minute and tell her everything!

He swung round and headed out to the hall. He was almost at the front door when it struck him that he couldn't go anywhere. He couldn't leave Tomàs on his own and he certainly couldn't ask Mrs Mackenzie to come back at this time of the night. It looked as though he would have to put off the moment once again.

Sighing with frustration, he opened the door and went into the bedroom where Tomàs was sleeping. He went to the bed and gazed down at the sleeping child, smiling when he saw how Tomàs was curled up into a ball, like a small animal. The child's skin was flushed with sleep, his black curls falling damply onto his forehead.

Morgan gently brushed them back, feeling his heart swelling with tenderness. Tomàs managed to touch him in ways that nobody else had done; the little boy aroused feelings that he hadn't believed himself capable of. However, he couldn't afford to let himself be influenced by them. He had to do what was best for Tomàs and he was afraid that agreeing to help with the adoption wouldn't be in the child's best interests. Maybe it would be simpler if he left things as they were and didn't say anything to Katrina. That wasn't being cowardly. It was just being sensible.

Katrina knew that something was wrong as soon as she woke the next morning. Surprisingly, she had slept well and hadn't stirred once during the night. However, there was no ignoring the air of tension that seemed to hang over the ward. When she spotted Maggie Carr passing, she called her over.

'What's going on?' she demanded.

Maggie glanced over her shoulder then lowered her

voice. 'Sandra has gone missing. There's going to be a terrific stink about it because nobody realised she had gone until this morning.'

'Really?' She couldn't hide her dismay. 'Surely somebody would have noticed her bed was empty?'

'Apparently not.' Maggie sighed. 'I suppose it was having agency nurses working here last night—they didn't know any of the patients and probably assumed that Sandra's bed was vacant. Anyway, keep it under your hat, will you? None of the patients are supposed to know.'

'I won't say anything,' Katrina agreed readily. She sighed as Maggie hurried away. What a to-do! Where on earth had Sandra got to and why had she done such a crazy thing?

It was all very puzzling but she feigned ignorance when a couple of the other patients asked her what was going on. She could understand the hospital's desire not to let the story gather momentum because it would be extremely bad for publicity. It was obvious that Morgan must have been informed about what had happened because he arrived shortly after eight o'clock, and looked very grim as he accompanied Sister to the office.

Luke took the ward round that day and Maggie accompanied him as Sister was busy. Katrina couldn't help feeling rather envious when she saw how Maggie and Luke behaved with each other. There was nothing overt about it, but it was obvious how much in love they were. She couldn't help thinking how lucky they were to have their future to look forward to.

That thought naturally made her think about her and Morgan so it was a relief when it was time to go to the physiotherapy unit for her daily session. She certainly wouldn't have time to brood while she was struggling with her exercises!

Graham Walker was also due for a Physio appointment that day so the porter took them down in the lift together and left them in the waiting room. It was obvious that he had heard about Sandra's disappearance and was extremely worried about her.

'I can't believe that she would do something so stupid,' he declared as they waited for the physiotherapists to collect them.

'Neither can I,' Katrina agreed. 'Heaven knows how much harm she could do to herself. Was that her husband who came to see her last night, by the way?'

'Yes.' Graham grimaced. 'I got the feeling he was less than pleased to find me talking to Sandra. That's why I made a hasty exit.'

'I see. Did she tell you anything while you were talking to her?'

'She was on the verge of it when her husband arrived.' Graham sighed. 'Something is seriously wrong there. I just have this feeling even though I can't explain it.'

The physiotherapist came to take him through for his treatment at that point so the conversation ended there. Katrina was taken into the unit a short time later. Because her fractured femur would take months to heal, it was imperative that her knee, ankle and foot were exercised regularly to prevent the joints stiffening. It was also vital to maintain mobility in the rest of her body because she was no longer getting sufficient exercise to keep her muscles toned. Regular physiotherapy was aimed at alleviating any problems.

It was extremely hard work and she was soon exhausted as the physiotherapist, Danny Price, put her through her exercise routine. She heaved a sigh as they came to the last exercise, which consisted of lifting a pair of hand-held weights level with her shoulders.

'I don't know if I've got the strength to do this,' she complained, mopping her damp face with the towel Danny had given her.

'Don't even think of quitting,' he warned. 'Otherwise I'll

double the number of lifts you have to do the next time you come!'

'Sadist!' she accused, grinning at him. She liked Danny because he managed to be both firm yet sympathetic. He was in his late forties and had told her at their first session that he'd been the physiotherapist for one of the major football clubs before he'd decided to switch to the far less lucrative NHS work so that he could help more people.

Now she dried her damp palms on the towel then picked up the weights. 'OK, ready when you are,' she began, then broke off as the telephone in the office rang.

'Saved by the bell,' Danny joked. He looked up as the door opened and laughed. 'Ah, maybe not.'

Katrina glanced round, feeling her pulse leap when she saw that Morgan had come into the room. He came over to them and nodded to Danny. 'I came to see how Katrina was doing. I hope you don't mind?'

'Not at all,' Danny replied cheerfully, winking at her. 'In fact, you chose the perfect moment. Katrina knows what she needs to do so you can supervise her while I answer the phone. And don't let her start slacking!'

'Cheek!' She pulled a face as Danny hurried to the office. 'I never slack and he knows it.'

Morgan smiled although she couldn't help noticing how tired he looked. 'Danny is a stickler but he gets the best out of his patients. That's why I asked specifically for him to take charge of your case.'

'Oh, I see.' She was touched by his concern and quickly busied herself with the weights so that he wouldn't notice.

Morgan stood beside her while she raised the weights parallel with her shoulders then lowered them to her sides. 'Try to keep your arms level for a little longer then lower them slowly,' he advised. 'It will help to strengthen the biceps and the flexors of the wrists and fingers.'

'I'll try.' She performed the exercise another couple of times before Danny reappeared.

'Sorry about this, Katrina,' he apologised. 'That was Roger Hopkins on the phone,' he explained, obviously concerned about the conversation he'd just had with the hospital's manager. 'He wants to have a word with me about a patient I've been working with who has gone missing apparently.'

'That's right,' Morgan confirmed. 'Roger said that he wanted to speak to everyone who's had dealings with Sandra Sullivan in the past week, to see if they have any idea where she might have gone.'

'I doubt whether I'll be able to tell him very much,' Danny said, frowning. 'She barely said a word to me even though we live in the same road.'

'Really?' Katrina exclaimed. 'Then you must know her husband?'

'Can't say that I do.' Danny grimaced. 'He keeps himself very much to himself, as Sandra does. I believe he works at the new technology park, but that's all I know about him. My wife and I did invite them round to a barbecue not long after they moved in but they made some sort of excuse.

'Anyway, I could go and see Roger now if you wouldn't mind staying here with Katrina,' he suggested, looking at Morgan. 'It would save me running late for the rest of the day.'

'Of course I'll stay,' Morgan agreed immediately. He waited until the door had closed before he turned to Katrina with a wicked grin. 'So what are you waiting for, young lady? I'm in charge now so get cracking and don't forget what I've told you either.'

'It's a good job we're not on board ship,' she grumbled, wiping her hands again on the towel. 'You'd be able to keelhaul me if I didn't perform to your exacting standards!'

'Temper, temper!' he replied, laughing. He perched on the edge of a bench as he waited for her to begin, and folded his arms across his chest. He wasn't wearing a jacket for once and the action pulled the cotton fabric of his shirt taut across his chest, providing a tantalising glimpse of crisp, dark body hair. Katrina felt a little knot of heat uncurl in her stomach and quickly looked away. Noticing things like that certainly wouldn't help!

Morgan was merciless as he put Katrina through the rest of her exercises, correcting her each time he wasn't completely happy with her performance. He even ran through the list to make sure that she had done everything when she had finished.

'I've done them all. Cross my heart and hope to die!'

'All right, I'll believe you,' he conceded grudgingly, putting the worksheet back into its folder.

'Thank heavens for that!' she moaned, letting her head drop back in exhaustion. Every bit of her was tingling thanks to the gruelling exercises and she felt as limp as a wet rag. She lifted her hair off the back of her neck and tried to fan herself. 'I'm so hot! I think I'm going to melt.'

'Have you got something to tie back your hair?' he suggested.

'No, I forgot to bring a band with me,' she confessed, fanning even harder.

'Let me see what I can find,' he offered, heading for the office. He came back a moment later with an elastic band and handed it to her.

'Thanks.' Katrina scooped her hair into a ponytail but her arms were trembling so hard from her exertions that she couldn't manage to twine the elastic band around it.

'Here, let me do it.' He took the band from her then combed his fingers through her hair to pull it back from her face.

She sat rigidly still, trying to ignore the signals that were flashing through her body. The feel of his hands had set up a chain reaction of responses which ranged from delight to pure fear. She loved feeling his fingers moving so gently over her skull but she was afraid that she was enjoying it *too* much!

'How does that feel? Not too tight?'

There was a huskiness in his voice that made the signals work all the harder as they translated the new message. Morgan was enjoying touching her as much as she was enjoying being touched. The realisation sent her mind spinning into overdrive.

'Katrina?'

Morgan bent forward to look at her when she didn't answer and she closed her eyes as she felt the warmth of his breath on her damp cheek. The desire to turn her head so that she could feel that sweet warmth on her lips was overpowering but she made herself resist. It would be such a small step from that point to the next, but too big a leap. One kiss could be classed as an accident but a second certainly couldn't. Did she really want to have to explain to him, or to herself, why she had wanted it to happen?

'It's fine. Thank you,' she said, quickly bending to pick up the towel and thus removing herself from temptation.

'Good.' He cleared his throat. 'I'd better get you back up to the ward, then.'

'Of course. You must be anxious to get home,' she replied politely as he escorted her to the door. 'It's a pity that you had to come to work on your day off.'

'Needs must, as the saying goes,' he replied evenly. 'And talking about needs, have you thought any more about staying with me after you leave here? It makes a great deal of sense, Katrina, because you're going to need someone to help you for a while.'

'And that someone should be you?' she queried, not sure she liked the rather impersonal way he had phrased it.

'Why not? It's no big deal after all. I'm merely offering you a helping hand.' He shrugged. 'You would do the same for me, I expect.'

'Of course,' she began.

'So that's settled, then.' He looked round as the lift arrived. 'Right, let's get you back upstairs then I can go home and fetch Tomàs. He's dying to see you.'

Before she knew what was happening, she found herself whisked into the lift and on her way back to the ward. Morgan handed her over to one of the nurses the minute they arrived then promptly took his leave. He barely gave her time to say goodbye let alone anything else.

Katrina had her lunch then lay down on her bed to rest, but her mind was too busy to relax. She had the uncomfortable feeling that she'd been *bulldozed* into agreeing to stay with him, but had no idea what to do about it. If she objected, he would want to know why and she wasn't sure what her reasons were. After all, she would have done the same for him if the situation had been reversed, as he had been so quick to point out.

She groaned. The truth was that staying with Morgan could cause major problems, but what was the alternative? Trying to look after a lively three-year-old on her own, with her leg in plaster? Talk about being between the devil and the deep blue sea!

CHAPTER NINE

THE next two weeks flew past. Morgan barely had time to draw breath most days. The recent closure of the surgical department at the Royal, a hospital some ten miles away from Dalverston, meant that the number of patients they saw had increased dramatically. Although steps were being taken to amalgamate the staff from both hospitals, inevitably there were problems that needed his attention.

He ended up taking work home rather than letting it eat into time that he needed to spend with his patients. Once Tomàs was in bed he worked late into the night, making sure that everything would run smoothly. It was extremely tiring, working such long hours, but the upside was that he didn't have time to worry about Katrina coming to stay at his flat. Frankly, the longer he could put off thinking about the problems it might cause the better!

Nevertheless, by the time Friday morning arrived Morgan was starting to feel distinctly frazzled. Katrina was being discharged the following day and there was no way that he could bury his head in the sand—or under a mountain of paperwork—any longer. He knew that he would be walking an emotional tightrope while Katrina was staying with him and it wasn't a pleasant prospect. Consequently, he had little sympathy to spare when Cheryl Rothwell, his junior registrar, stumbled through a new patient's history during the morning ward round.

'Mrs Wilson suffered a Monteggia's fracture, Dr Rothwell,' he corrected coldly. 'Unless the human race has undergone some skeletal changes that I am unaware of, it means that the patient's ulna, the bone on the *inner* side of her forearm, was fractured just below the elbow, whilst the radius, the bone on the *outer* side, was dislocated from the elbow joint. Is that clear now?'

'Yes, sir, perfectly clear. Thank you,' Cheryl replied, her face flaming.

Morgan sighed when he saw Mrs Wilson mouth ''Never mind, dear'' to the young doctor as they moved away from the bed. He knew that he had been rather sharp with Cheryl and also knew what had prompted it. He glanced across the aisle and felt his heart give an all too familiar lurch when he saw that Katrina was watching him. There was a second when their eyes held before she looked away, but he'd seen the colour that had bloomed in her cheeks and his heart gave another few unsettling bounces.

Katrina was as aware of him as he was of her, and that was going to make the situation even more volatile in the coming weeks. However, he couldn't withdraw his invitation, neither did he want to, if he was honest. He just needed to find a way to…to *cope*, but it certainly wasn't going to be easy.

The rest of the round progressed smoothly, thankfully. Although Cheryl was rather subdued, she didn't sulk about the reprimand and Morgan was pleased that she had taken it so well. She would be a good doctor once she gained more confidence, and he made a note to tell her that when he had the chance. When they reached Katrina's bed, he turned to Cheryl once again.

'Bearing in mind the injury that Mrs Grey sustained, what would you expect to find by this point in her recovery?'

'There should have been some new bone growth by now, although it will be some months before healing is complete,' Cheryl replied promptly. She took the X-rays from the file and studied them for a moment then passed them to him.

'These were taken yesterday in readiness for your wife's…for Mrs Grey's discharge,' she quickly amended

'As you can see, sir, there's some new growth of callus already visible.'

Morgan held the X-rays up to the light while he tried to contain the rush of pleasure he'd felt on hearing Katrina referred to as his wife. Technically it had been correct, of course, although morally she couldn't be classed as such any longer. However, that didn't negate the fact that he'd experienced a certain thrill just now, and it worried him. A lot.

'That looks fine. Dr Fabrizzi did an excellent job and I'm not anticipating any problems,' he said formally, calling himself every kind of a fool. It would be difficult enough to find a balance in the coming weeks, and impossible if he let his mind start running away with him!

'So you're going to let me leave tomorrow as planned?' Katrina asked quietly.

Morgan handed back the X-rays before he turned to her. Maybe it was his imagination but the air seemed charged with tension all of a sudden. He felt his nerves tighten that bit more when he saw the pulse that was beating so betrayingly at the base of her throat. It was obvious that Katrina was every bit as on edge as he was, and suddenly all he wanted was to reassure her.

'I can't see any reason to keep you here,' he replied gravely. 'So long as you don't try doing too much, and give your leg a chance to heal properly, there should be no problems.'

She smiled up at him, her hazel eyes full of amusement all of a sudden. 'Then it's a good job that I'm going to have someone to tend to my every need, isn't it?'

Morgan felt his stomach sink as the comment hit home. He couldn't believe that he'd given no real thought to the full extent of the help that she would need in the coming weeks. Oh, he had dealt with the practicalities by arranging for Mrs Mackenzie to continue coming in daily to help look after Tomàs, but he hadn't even *considered* all the other things that Katrina wouldn't be able to do for herself, like bathing and dressing, for instance. It was an effort to hide his dismay when he realised that she was waiting for him to say something.

'The more you rest that leg, the faster it will heal,' he said gruffly.

He swung round and was disconcerted to find that Cheryl and Armand were watching him with interest. It was obvious that they had sensed that something was wrong, and it simply threw him even further off balance. It was a relief when a nurse came hurrying over to tell him that he was needed urgently in Theatre.

'Take over, please, Dr St Juste,' he instructed crisply, delighted to have the perfect excuse to make his escape. He wasn't used to people guessing when something had upset him so consequently he wasn't sure how to handle the situation. 'Everything should be quite straightforward from here on, but if you do have any problems, page me.'

'*Mais oui.*' Armand smiled graciously as he led the party to the next bed. Morgan saw Cheryl whisper something to the young French-Canadian doctor, heard them both laugh and quickly turned away. He didn't need a crystal ball to know that they were discussing him! Had his loss of composure been so obvious?

It was an effort to put that unsettling thought out of his head as he made his way to Theatres. It didn't help that it was ravelled up with so many others either. He couldn't believe that he had given no thought to how Katrina was going to manage with her personal care when she moved into the flat. It was only when he saw the grim expression on Luke Fabrizzi's face when they met up outside the locker room that he managed to collect himself.

'What's happened?' he demanded, leading the way into the room.

'Sandra Sullivan is on her way up from A and E,' Luke

told him tersely. 'They called me down because they were so worried about her.'

'How did it happen?' Morgan asked as he stripped off his jacket and started to change into scrubs.

'The police think that she's been beaten up and I'd say they were right. She's got fractures to both arms and all her fingers have been broken as well. Not your usual kind of injuries, by any means.' Luke's tone was bleak. 'It also looks as though her sternum has been damaged again, which is why A and E were so concerned.'

'Hell!' Morgan's voice crackled with fury. He dragged on a pair of baggy, cotton trousers and tightened the drawstring at his waist. 'Do the police have any idea who's responsible?'

'They're looking for her husband, apparently.'

'Then let's hope they find him,' Morgan replied darkly.

Dave Carson had the patient fully anaesthetised by the time he and Luke entered Theatre. Morgan went straight to the operating table, feeling a wave of anger wash over him as he took stock of Sandra's battered body. If he lived to be a hundred, he would never understand how one human being could do this to another!

He took a deep breath. It wasn't his job to worry about things like that. His job was to put the pieces back together and make sure that the patient was given the best chance possible of recovering. Once that was done, his role would come to an end.

Except it wasn't that simple, was it? Nobody could deal with a situation like this and remain untouched by it. Not even him.

Morgan felt a shiver ripple down his spine. He had always been able to detach himself emotionally in the past but he was no longer able to do that. It was as though the barriers which he had erected between himself and the world had started to break down.

It was hard enough to face that fact, but even more dif-

ficult to accept why it was happening. Having Katrina come
back into his life had been the catalyst. Her return had set
off a chain reaction so that slowly but surely everything
was changing.

The thought scared him stiff. How was he going to put
his life back together after she left?

Katrina was all packed and ready to leave way before the
time Morgan had arranged to collect her on Saturday morning. She had to admit that she was growing increasingly
nervous as the minutes ticked away. Had she done the right
thing by agreeing to stay with him?

She sighed. She must have asked herself that question a
thousand times in the past week, but she still wasn't sure.
All she knew was that the alternative wasn't any better!

'Why so miserable? Don't tell me you're going to miss
being here?'

She summoned a smile when Beatrice Bosanko stopped
by her bed. 'I won't. Well, I'll miss some things, of course.
I've really enjoyed getting to know you and the other
nurses, Beatrice.'

'And we've enjoyed having you,' Beatrice replied with
a grin. 'It's not often that we have a patient who is so co-
operative, not to mention one who is so *interesting*!'

Katrina rolled her eyes. 'Mmm, I think the only interesting thing has been my link with Morgan. Am I right or
am I right?'

Beatrice gave a booming laugh. 'You're right. It's been
a revelation, finding out that man is human.' She obviously
realised how tactless that might have been because she hurried on. 'Did Dr Grey tell you the news, by the way?'

'What news?' Katrina queried. She hadn't seen Morgan
since yesterday's ward round. He had sent a message to say
that he wouldn't be able to visit her the previous night
although Mrs Mackenzie had brought Tomàs in to see her.

She had been a little put out by his absence, if she was

honest, although she had tried to hide it from her visitors. It had crossed her mind that he might have been having second thoughts about her staying with him, but she had quickly dismissed the idea. Morgan had had ample opportunity to change his mind if he'd wanted to.

'Sandra Sullivan is in Intensive Care. She's in a bad way, too.' Beatrice lowered her voice. 'I met Lee Anderson in the canteen and he told me that she'd been beaten up. The police are looking for her husband, apparently.'

'No! Oh, how dreadful.' Katrina gasped as everything suddenly fell into place. 'Maybe he's done it before and that's why she didn't want anyone getting in touch with him after her accident. It all makes sense now, doesn't it?'

'It does, unfortunately,' Beatrice agreed. 'If only she'd told us what had been going on, maybe we could have helped.'

'Maybe she found it too difficult to admit what he'd been doing to her. A lot of women who are abused are unable to speak about their experiences,' she said sadly.

'So I believe.' The nurse glanced round when she heard footsteps approaching the bed and smiled. 'Ah, here's Dr Grey now and your little boy. He's such a poppet, isn't he?'

'He is,' Katrina agreed, holding out her arms for a hug as Tomàs came racing to her. 'Hello, darling, how are you?' she began, but before she could repeat the question in Spanish, Tomàs answered her.

'Very well, thank you,' he replied, grinning delightedly when she gasped.

'You clever boy! Who taught you to say that?' she demanded, giving him another hug.

'Papa.' Tomàs grasped hold of Morgan's hand as he came to join them, and Katrina felt a lump come to her throat when she saw the trust in the child's eyes as he proudly repeated the phrase for Morgan's benefit.

'Well done!' Morgan smiled as he tousled the child's black curls. *'Bien hecho!'*

Katrina laughed. 'It sounds as though both of you are making excellent progress.'

'Tomàs is doing far better than I am, but we're learning from each other,' he explained levelly. 'So, are you all packed and ready to go, then?'

Katrina nodded, feeling suddenly nervous now that the time had arrived. She still wasn't sure if she'd made the right decision but it was too late to change her mind.

'I...I didn't have all that much so everything fitted into the case. Mrs Mackenzie brought it in for me last night, along with the clothes you'd found for me to wear.' She glanced down at the lemon sweatshirt and camel jersey skirt she was wearing. 'I was worried whether I'd be able to get any of my clothes over this cast, but this skirt is perfect. I even managed to get dressed all by myself for once.'

'Good,' he said brusquely.

Katrina frowned when she saw the rather grim expression that crossed his face as he picked up the case. Something had obviously upset him, although she had no idea what it could be. All she'd done had been to thank him for finding her something suitable to wear! It was all very puzzling, but before she could ask him what was wrong, a porter arrived with a wheelchair to take her down in the lift.

Morgan followed with Tomàs as she was wheeled down the ward. They paused briefly by the desk so that she could thank the staff for their kindness then they were on their way. Katrina gasped when they left the building and she discovered a private ambulance waiting outside for them. 'You shouldn't have gone to all this trouble,' she exclaimed as the crew helped her on board.

'I thought it would be easier than trying to get you and that cast into my car. Why struggle when there's no need?'

She smiled warmly, touched by his thoughtfulness. 'Well, it was kind of you, Morgan. Thank you.'

It didn't take them long to reach their destination and Morgan kept up an easy, undemanding conversation all the way there. Katrina sensed that he was trying to put her at ease and she was grateful for that. However, she couldn't deny that she was a bag of nerves by the time the ambulance crew had got her settled on the sofa in the sitting-room. It was a relief when Morgan disappeared to see the men out because it meant that she had a few minutes to compose herself.

She took a deep breath then deliberately took stock of the huge, airy room, hoping that it would help to take the edge off her nervousness if she concentrated on her surroundings. A frown pleated her brow as her eyes skimmed over the vast expanse of pale, wooden flooring, the starkly white ceiling and walls. The room was a complete surprise—she couldn't help comparing it to the rooms in the house where they'd lived after their marriage. The decor there had been quite traditional, but Morgan had opted for a very modern look this time.

She found herself wondering if it had been a conscious decision as she took stock of the white leather sofa and matching chair, the stainless-steel shelving unit built along one wall, the granite-topped coffee-tables. Had he purposely chosen a style that wouldn't remind him of their old home, perhaps?

'How about a cup of tea, or maybe coffee if you'd prefer?' Morgan had come back into the room without her noticing and she jumped.

'Oh, tea would be nice,' she said quickly, hating the fact that her pulse had started racing again. She took another calming breath as he left to make the drinks. Life would be extremely difficult if she started jumping like a startled kitten every time he appeared. She had to calm down and try to relax, make herself at home…

Katrina sighed. That was the *last* thing she must do! She must never forget that she was simply a guest in this flat. Morgan had invited her to stay purely out of a sense of duty, not because he'd wanted her there. It was odd how painful she found that thought.

Fortunately, he came back with the tea just then so she was able to push it to the back of her mind. He moved a table closer to the sofa and put her cup on it, then unloaded a second cup and a glass of orange juice from the tray.

'Where's Tomàs got to?' he asked, glancing round.

'I'll go and see,' she replied, automatically starting to rise.

'I'll find him. You stay there.' He pressed her back into the seat then went to find the little boy. Katrina looked round when she heard a loud exclamation followed by gurgles of childish laughter coming from the hall.

'What's going on?' she asked as Morgan came back, carrying a giggling Tomàs over his shoulder.

'This little horror was hiding behind the door.' He swung the child down to the floor then bent and tickled him. 'I'll teach you to jump out and scare me to half to death, you little wretch!'

Tomàs squirmed around the floor, shrieking with laughter as Morgan tickled him. Katrina found herself smiling as well because the child's joy was so contagious. She glanced at Morgan and felt a wealth of sadness fill her when she saw his smiling face. It was obvious how much he enjoyed being with the child yet he would deny himself that pleasure as a matter of principle.

It made her wonder all of a sudden why he was so against the idea of adoption—not just helping her to adopt Tomàs, but adoption in general. She had never really thought about it before, but suddenly it struck her that he had never really explained his objections whenever the subject had come up in the past. Now she had the strangest feeling that it was important that she find out.

'You should be resting and here we are making all this noise.' Morgan frowned when she looked blankly at him. 'I expect you're tired and that's why you're so quiet.'

'A bit, although I don't know why.' She summoned a smile, deeming it safer to go along with the assumption rather than admit what she'd been thinking. If she wanted him to tell her why he was so opposed to the idea of adoption, she needed to choose the right moment, and this wasn't it. 'I've hardly done a thing for the past three weeks so I've no excuse, really.'

'You'll find that you tire easily for a while because your body is still trying to cope with the after-effects of the accident,' he explained.

'I expect you're right.' She drank her tea then looked up in surprise when he took the cup from her.

'How about lying down and resting for an hour? I promised Tomàs that I would take him to the farm to see the donkeys, so you'll have a bit of peace with us out of the way.'

'Oh, I don't know if I should,' she began, because it didn't seem fair that Morgan should have to entertain the little boy when she was there.

'Of course you should!' He shook his head when she went to argue. 'The whole point of you being here, Katrina, is so that you can rest. Come along now. I won't take no for an answer.'

He helped her up from the sofa before she could summon up any more objections. Looping his arm around her waist, he took most of her weight. 'Do you think you can make it as far as the bedroom? I can carry you if—'

'No!' She flushed when she felt his start of surprise at her vehement refusal. However, the last thing she wanted was Morgan carrying her to bed. She bit her lip, refusing to think about all the times when he'd done exactly that.

'You always were far too independent,' he said flatly. Katrina could hear the undercurrent in his voice and knew immediately that he, too, had been remembering those other occasions when he hadn't needed to ask her permission, but had simply swept her into his arms and carried her to bed. It brought it home to her just how volatile the situation was. Nobody could totally erase their memories even if they wanted to. She and Morgan certainly hadn't been able to.

'I'm afraid that you and Tomàs will have to share,' he explained, elbowing the bedroom door open. 'I rarely have visitors so there didn't seem any point in buying a place with too many spare bedrooms.'

'It's fine, really,' she assured him, pleased to hear that her own voice had sounded deceptively level. She sank onto the bed and looked around, giving herself a few moments' breathing space. Here, too, the furnishings were extremely modern and rather stark. However, there were rows of Tomàs's pictures taped to the walls and they added a splash of colour.

'I see Tomàs has made his mark on the place already,' she observed lightly, feeling a little easier. There were bound to be problems initially but once she and Morgan had adapted to the situation, they would cope.

'He loves drawing, doesn't he? We get through reams of paper. Still, they do add a bit of colour to the place. I keep meaning to decorate but I never seem to get the chance, working all the time.'

He shrugged as he looked around the room. 'This was the show flat so I took the easy option and bought everything lock, stock and barrel, although it isn't really my taste.'

'Oh, I see! I thought—' She broke off as she realised what she'd been going to say. The last thing she wanted was to start reminding him about the past again.

'You thought what?' he prompted. 'Come on, Katrina, what were you going to say before you thought better of it? Life will be extremely difficult if we feel that we need to watch every word we say to each other.'

She felt a little knot of tension grip her when she heard the challenge in his voice. Maybe it was silly to respond to it but she had done nothing to be ashamed of. 'That you must have chosen the decor deliberately because it's so different to our old house.'

'It wasn't my choice, as I said,' he replied shortly. 'The architects decided how they wanted the place to look and that was that. Anyway, I'd better let you rest now. Do you need anything before I go out?'

'No. I'm fine, thank you.'

She sighed as he left the room. It was obvious that he hadn't been pleased by that remark but he'd been the one who'd said that they shouldn't monitor what they said.

Still, maybe she should be a little more careful in future. There was no point in making life difficult. She would be the perfect guest—polite, courteous, never too obtrusive—and concentrate all her energies on getting better.

That was the most important thing, that she was well enough to carry on with her plans to adopt Tomàs. If Morgan wouldn't help her, she might have a difficult job convincing the British authorities that the little boy should be allowed to remain in the country. There had been a number of high-profile adoption cases involving children from abroad recently, and the authorities were being extra careful and demanding that all the criteria were met. Not that anything was going to stop her adopting Tomàs. No, come what may, he was going to be her son!

She lay down and closed her eyes, wishing that she could blot out her thoughts as easily as she had blotted out the light. It was fruitless wishing that the child could have been Morgan's son as well. Some dreams were destined never to come true, although that didn't stop people dreaming, of course.

CHAPTER TEN

THE day had gone surprisingly well so that Morgan was in a much more positive frame of mind when he closed the bedroom door after putting an exhausted Tomàs to bed on Saturday night. Admittedly, he and Katrina hadn't spent very much time on their own with Tomàs there, but it had been less of a strain than he had feared. It made him wonder if he had been foolish to worry so much. After all, he and Katrina were two sensible adults so surely they would find a way to cope during the coming weeks.

Katrina was sitting on the sofa again when he went back to the sitting-room, her injured leg propped on a stool. The rest had done her good because there was a bit more colour in her face than there had been earlier in the day. It made him wonder if she, too, had been worrying herself to death about how they would manage, living together in the flat. Hopefully, she was feeling a bit more confident about it now.

'He's fast asleep so how about a glass of wine?' he suggested when she looked up. 'I think we deserve one, don't you?'

'That would be nice. I can't remember the last time I had a glass of wine that was actually *drinkable*!'

'Really?' He studied her curiously, wondering what she'd meant.

'The local priest in the village near where we were working made his own wine,' she explained with a grin. 'He insisted that anyone who went to visit him had a glass, and it was absolutely awful. I don't know what he made it from, but it was so strong that it almost stripped the enamel off your teeth!'

He laughed. 'Sounds like an experience to be missed. Anyway, I promise you that this wine won't give your dentist nightmares. I'll just go and open a bottle.'

He left the room and went to the kitchen. He'd forgotten to ask if she wanted red or white but decided that it probably didn't matter. If she'd been drinking home brew then anything would taste good after that!

He opened a bottle of white wine and took it back to the sitting-room along with some glasses. Katrina had her eyes closed and her head resting against the cushions while she listened to a CD that he had put on earlier.

'This is nice,' she murmured, without opening her eyes. 'Who is it?'

'An Irish band—they've had a number of hit records in the past couple of years,' he explained, setting the glasses on a coffee-table while he filled them.

'I can understand why. That girl's voice is just beautiful.' She opened her eyes and sighed. 'I've a lot of catching up to do from the look of it. I've no idea who's in the charts or who's written the latest bestseller. The area where I was working was very remote so we didn't get much news from home.'

'It must have been a big change for you working in a place like that after London,' he observed, handing her one of the glasses.

'It was. A real culture shock at first, in fact.' She took a sip of the wine and sighed blissfully. 'This is gorgeous!'

'Not too strong?' he teased as he sat down on the chair.

'You've no idea what strong means until you've tasted Father Ignatius's home brew,' she retorted. 'One of the other nurses tried using it as paint stripper and it worked!'

Morgan chuckled. 'It's a miracle that you survived to tell the tale from the sound of it.'

Morgan drank some of the wine then looked at her curiously. All of a sudden he realised that he wanted to know more about what she'd been doing during the years they'd spent apart. 'It sounds as though you had some fun while you were working in South America. It wasn't all bad, then?'

'It certainly wasn't,' she assured him. 'Oh, it was very stressful at times because the kids we saw weren't always easy to deal with. A lot of them sniffed glue or other substances, so you had to be careful because of how they might react. But there were bright spots in even the darkest days, something to laugh about and keep you going when you were feeling down.'

'I can't imagine what it must have been like.' He took a deep breath because the thought of the danger she had been in at times made him feel all churned up inside. How would he have coped if he'd known what she was doing? he wondered darkly. Could he have slept at night, knowing that she had been putting herself at risk to help those children?

He realised that she'd said something and frowned. 'Sorry, what was that?'

'I was just wondering why you decided to move out of London.' Katrina shrugged. 'It must have been a big change for you, too, moving up here. What made you decide to take the plunge?'

'It was too good an opportunity to miss,' he replied neutrally, not wanting to explain that he hadn't been able to bear being in London when everywhere he went he'd been reminded of their life together. 'Dalverston General had been named as a centre of excellence for a number of specialities, orthopaedic surgery being one of them. It meant that I would have a virtually free hand, setting things up the way I wanted them.'

'A golden opportunity,' she agreed flatly.

'It was.' He frowned, wondering if he had imagined that rather wistful note in her voice. 'I certainly haven't regretted making the move. Dalverston is a good place to live and I've been very fortunate with my colleagues. It's just a shame that Luke won't be staying.'

'He's leaving Dalverston? I didn't know that,' she exclaimed.

'He and Maggie are moving to Boston after their wedding next month,' he explained. 'Luke has a consultant's post lined up there so I can't blame him for wanting to go back, even though I shall miss working with him.'

'So that means you'll have more changes to contend with in your professional life as well as in your private life?'

'I expect I'll survive,' he said shortly, picking up the bottle to top up their glasses.

'Oh, I'm sure you will, Morgan.'

Once again there seemed to be a wistful note in her voice. He knew that it was probably foolish to ask her what was wrong but he couldn't resist. 'Has something upset you, Katrina?'

'Of course not,' she denied a shade too sharply. She picked up her glass again. 'This really *is* delicious.'

'I'm glad you like it,' he said politely. Despite her assertions to the contrary, he knew that something had upset her. The idea disturbed him so much that he wasn't as careful as he might otherwise have been. 'The one good thing that my stepfather ever did for me was to teach me how to chose a decent bottle of wine. At least I've got something to be grateful to him for.'

He could have bitten off his tongue the moment he'd said that. He never spoke about his stepfather and could scarcely believe that he'd mentioned him now. He felt his pulse leap when he heard Katrina put down her glass with a small thud that seemed to reverberate around the room.

'What did you mean by that, Morgan? Why was it the one good thing that your stepfather ever did for you?'

'It was just a figure of speech, that's all,' he said brusquely.

'Really? And you expect me to believe that, do you?' She uttered a scornful laugh. 'Come on, Morgan. You didn't hear yourself just now. I don't think I've ever heard such loathing in anyone's voice!'

'You're imagining things.'

He stood up abruptly and went to the window, unable to sit there a moment longer. He couldn't believe that he'd said something so revealing, yet why should it surprise him when that period in his life had been on his mind such a lot lately? Hadn't he decided at one point that he should tell her about it, before he'd had second thoughts?

'I'm not imagining anything, Morgan. I *know* what I heard. I also know how reluctant you always were to talk about your family. Why? What's the big secret? Why won't you tell me?'

He felt his heart ache with a searing pain when he heard the concern in her voice. 'Because there's nothing to tell you. You know that my father died when I was a baby and that my mother remarried when I was ten. They're both dead now so what else is there to say?' He shrugged. 'It's ancient history and has no bearing at all on the present situation.'

'Doesn't it? You're absolutely sure about that, are you, Morgan?' Her hazel eyes flashed with anger as he glanced round. 'We're all products of our childhoods so what makes you any different?'

'I never claimed that I was different,' he shot back impatiently. 'You're reading far too much into a chance remark, Katrina.'

'Maybe I am, but maybe it's time that I asked questions like that. Maybe I should have asked them earlier, in fact.'

'I have no idea what you're talking about,' he began, but she didn't give him time to finish.

'Why are you so opposed to the idea of adoption? I don't just mean helping me to adopt Tomàs—that's different. But the whole idea of adopting a child.' She took a quick breath that made her breasts rise and fall beneath the soft lemon sweatshirt and he could tell how agitated she was. 'When we found out that you couldn't father a child, the doctor at the clinic suggested that we should think about adopting, but you refused to consider it. Why, Morgan? I need to know.'

'It simply never appealed to me,' he said shortly, praying that she couldn't tell how much it hurt him to have to lie even if it was only by omission. To say that the idea of adopting a child hadn't appealed was an understatement—it had been the last thing he would have considered, although the idea didn't seem nearly as abhorrent now as it had done four years ago...

He brushed aside that dangerous thought because he simply couldn't deal with it at that moment. Katrina was still watching him and he knew that he had to find a way to make her understand.

'The main reason why I wanted a child so much was because it would have been our child, the child we had conceived together. It wouldn't have been the same if we'd adopted one.'

'Do you think I didn't understand that? I felt the same, Morgan. I wanted your baby so much that it almost broke my heart when I found out that it was never going to happen.'

He saw her eyes fill with tears and bit back an oath as he realised that he should have found a better way to phrase that. He crossed the room and crouched in front of her, hating himself when he saw the stricken expression on her face.

'I didn't mean to upset you. That was never my intention.'

'I know.' She summoned a wobbly smile as she brushed the tears from her cheeks. 'I suppose I'm just rather keyed up at the moment with the accident and everything else that has happened lately.'

'I expect you are. It's been a difficult few weeks, hasn't it, Katrina?' he said softly.

'It has.' She took a deep breath then let it out on a sigh. 'We were doing so well, too. We'd managed to get through the day without too many hiccups.'

'So you were as worried as I was?' he teased, striving to lighten the mood. It hurt unbearably to see her so distressed, although he was a little surprised that she had got so upset after all this time.

'You—worried? You could have fooled me,' she retorted, doing her best to rise to the occasion.

'You mean I managed to hide it *that* well?' Morgan smiled when she laughed shakily. 'Hmm, I didn't think so. I might be able to fool most of the people most of the time, but I have never been able to fool you.'

'I'm glad.' She cupped his cheek with her hand and her eyes were full of something that made his blood start to race through his veins, something that made his heart swell and filled him with a feeling of longing so intense, so fierce, that if he hadn't been crouching down he might very well have fallen to his knees. 'I would hate to think that you had shut me out completely, Morgan.'

Her hand lingered against his cheek for a moment before she let it fall to her side and there was a deliberately upbeat note in her voice now. 'Anyway, I think I'll have an early night, if you don't mind. I don't know why I should be so tired after having that rest earlier in the day. Maybe it's the wine.'

'It could be.' He stood and helped her to her feet, steeling himself as she leant against him for support. It was the sweetest kind of torment to hold her like that, to feel her soft curves pressed against his side, to smell the scent of her skin. It was a test of his self-control he could have done without, but he was determined not to do anything else to upset her that night.

He helped her into the bedroom, wondering if she would be able to get undressed by herself, wondering what he would do if she asked him for help. Could he trust himself not to take advantage of her vulnerable state? For the first time in his adult life, he wasn't sure if he was in control of himself!

'Goodnight, Morgan. I'll see you in the morning.'

It was a dismissal, clear and simple, and he felt a wave of relief wash over him that he wouldn't be put to the test. 'Goodnight,' he echoed, quickly leaving the room and closing the door.

He went back to the sitting-room and poured himself another glass of wine then went to the window. Night had drawn in and the town was a mass of twinkling lights, like jewels sprinkled across black velvet.

Morgan stared at them until his vision blurred, until he could no longer see through the veil of tears in his eyes. Four years' worth of pain and heartache, of loss and grief poured from him as he stood there, and when it was over he knew that he would remember this moment all his life. It was when he had finally faced the truth.

He would never stop loving Katrina until the day he died.

Sunday had been such a strain that Katrina was relieved when Monday arrived. Although Morgan had treated her with impeccable courtesy she couldn't have failed to notice how distant he had been. She'd sensed that he'd been deliberately trying to put up a barrier between them, and it had hurt to know that she was responsible for it.

She had lain awake most of Saturday night, going over and over everything that had been said, but she still hadn't found an answer to that question she'd asked him. The only person who could tell her why he was so opposed to the idea of adoption was Morgan himself, and there seemed even less chance than ever of that happening. When he came into the kitchen on Monday morning, dressed for work, she couldn't help wishing that she had never raised the subject in the first place. It certainly hadn't achieved anything, although, deep down, she knew that it was the key to everything.

'Mrs Mackenzie will be here at eight so there's no need to worry about tidying up,' he explained as he poured himself a cup of coffee. 'I've asked her to make lunch for you and Tomàs then take him to the park this afternoon while you rest.'

'I have a physio session this afternoon,' she reminded him, trying not to feel hurt by his tone. Morgan was treating her the same as he might have treated a casual guest—politely, courteously, *unfeelingly*.

'I'd forgotten about that,' he said shortly as he put down the cup and went to the phone. 'I'll arrange for a taxi to pick you and take you home again afterwards.'

'There's no need,' she said sharply. 'An ambulance will be coming for me. It's all arranged.'

She looked round as Tomàs came hurtling into the room, glad of an excuse to put an end to the overly polite exchange. Maybe Morgan felt that this was the best way to handle the situation after Saturday night but she knew that it would be a tremendous strain on both of them if he kept it up.

Fortunately, she had no time to dwell on that unhappy thought because Tomàs was clamouring for her attention. By the time she'd got him settled with a bowl of cereal and a glass of orange juice Morgan had finished his coffee and was ready to leave.

'I'd better be off, then. If you need me, phone my office and leave a message with my secretary. She'll be able to track me down.'

'I'll be fine,' she assured him, forcing a smile. 'Mrs Mackenzie will be here soon, and I've got Tomàs to keep me company so I won't have a chance to get bored.'

'Just don't try doing too much,' he warned, frowning. 'You need to rest that leg as much as possible.'

'Yes, Doctor,' she retorted. 'I'm not a complete idiot,

you know. I promise you that I wasn't planning on going for a ten-mile hike with this thing on my leg.'

She glared at the cast, feeling suddenly impatient with herself. She hated to feel so…so *helpless*! She looked up when she heard Morgan laugh, feeling her heart starting to thunder inside her when she saw the amusement in his eyes.

'I wouldn't put it past you, Katrina. I know what a very determined woman you are!'

Her mouth quirked into a slight smile as she felt a rush of warmth invade her. Maybe it was crazy to have let a smile affect her so much but it was just so wonderful to see it after the aloofness he had shown towards her the day before. 'Why do I have a nasty feeling that wasn't meant as a compliment?'

'Probably because you have an overly suspicious mind.' He treated her to another warm smile before he seemed to realise what he had done. She felt her heart contract on a spasm of pain as she saw a veil come down over his eyes once more. She barely managed to reply as he said a curt goodbye because it hurt so much. Morgan was deliberately shutting her out and she couldn't bear the thought that he could treat her like a stranger after all they had meant to each other.

It was a relief when Mrs Mackenzie arrived a few minutes later because it meant that she didn't have time to brood. It turned out that Mrs Mackenzie had been a nurse many years before, at a small cottage hospital in her native Scotland. Lack of funding had meant that the staff had learned to improvise with the equipment that was available, a talent that now proved invaluable. Katrina was delighted when the houseckeeper devised a method for her to take a shower with the help of a stool placed in the shower stall and several plastic bin liners.

'That was wonderful!' she declared as the elderly woman helped her dry off. 'I only managed a sponge bath yesterday and, although it meant that I was clean, it really wasn't the same as having a proper shower.'

'Och, it just takes a bit of working out, that's all,' Mrs Mackenzie declared, briskly shaking out a towel. 'Now, let me dry your back then you can get yourself dressed. Maybe the wee laddie can help you?'

Katrina laughed as Tomàs clapped his hands in delight at the idea. 'I'm amazed how much English he's picked up since he's been with you. Have you been teaching him?'

'The odd word, but it's Dr Grey who's mainly responsible. He's spent hours playing with him.' Mrs Mackenzie smiled as she helped Katrina up. 'Maybe I shouldn't say this, but it's done Dr Grey the power of good because he's not nearly as withdrawn as he used to be. He's a completely different person, in fact, although that might be because you're back, not just because of Thomas being here.'

Katrina didn't say anything although she couldn't help but see the meaningful look the housekeeper gave her. She let Mrs Mackenzie help her to the bedroom, trying not to dwell on what she'd heard. She sighed as she sent Tomàs to fetch one of the clean sweatshirts Morgan had given her from the drawer. Maybe Morgan *had* been behaving differently of late but she doubted if the change had been permanent after the way he'd acted the day before and that morning.

The ambulance arrived shortly after one o'clock to collect her. She found a couple of other patients on board when the crew helped her inside. Dalverston General offered a first-rate service to its patients, and ferrying them back and forth to outpatient appointments was all part of the high level of care they provided. They picked up two more people *en route* before they arrived at the hospital well in time for her appointment.

'Thank you.' Katrina smiled as the crew got her a wheelchair for the transfer to the physiotherapy department. They pushed her into reception area then left her there to wait for a porter to take her through. She was just wishing that she had brought a magazine with her to read to while away the time when the swing doors opened and she saw Maggie Carr coming into the building.

'This is a surprise. How are you?' She glanced at the carrier bags Maggie was carrying and grinned. 'Is there anything left in the shops?'

'Not much!' Maggie plonked the bags on the floor and groaned. 'I'm *shattered*. I never realised just how exhausting shopping could be, and I still have an eight-hour shift to work on top of it!'

'You should have gone on your day off,' Katrina advised.

'I know. It's just that I don't seem to have enough time to get everything done. There are just three weeks to go before the wedding and you wouldn't believe how much there is to do.' She picked up one of the bags. 'Still, I've solved one problem, the most important one to my mind, too.'

Katrina gasped when she saw the delicate confection of cream satin and lace. 'Oh, that is just so gorgeous! Where on earth did you find it?'

'A new boutique that's just opened in town. They have the most wonderful lingerie there.' Maggie held the nightgown against her and smiled dreamily. 'I hope Luke likes it.'

'I don't think you need to worry about that,' Katrina said immediately. 'It's absolutely stunning.'

'It is, and such a change to the first nightgown he saw me wearing,' Maggie said, chuckling as she folded the nightdress and popped it back in the bag.

'You can't leave it there,' Katrina protested. 'You have to explain that remark.' She looked round as a porter appeared to take her to the physiotherapy unit. 'Oh, drat, now I'm not going to have a chance to hear the story!'

'I can take you to the physio department,' Maggie offered. 'I've another half-hour before I'm on duty.'

She quickly explained what was happening to the porter then picked up the bags and dumped them on Katrina's lap. 'You can carry those while I push you.'

'Sounds like a fair trade to me,' she agreed, laughing. 'So come on, tell me all about the first time Luke saw you in your night attire.'

'Night attire was right,' Maggie declared pithily. 'Luke stayed the night at my flat, you see. Oh, it was all very innocent because we weren't involved at the time,' she added hurriedly, then laughed when Katrina raised her brows.

'It's the truth, honestly! Anyway, I never gave any thought to what I was wearing so the next morning Luke was met by the sight of me wearing this nightshirt my brothers had bought for me with the immortal words I HATE MORNINGS BUT I'M GREAT IN BED emblazoned across the front. It's a wonder he didn't run a mile!'

'Oh, fabulous! I can just imagine your face. It must have been a picture!' Katrina laughed so hard that her eyes started to water then all of a sudden she found that she was crying in earnest.

'Hey, come on now. What's wrong?' Maggie steered the wheelchair into an alcove and bent to look at her. 'It wasn't such a dreadful tale, was it?'

'No.' She tried to smile. 'I'm sorry. I don't know what's the matter with me.'

'Don't you?' Maggie's tone was wry. 'I'd say it was obvious what was wrong. It's Morgan, isn't it?'

'No, of course not,' Katrina began, then sighed when she realised how pointless it was to lie. 'It's all such a mess. I wish I'd never come to Dalverston in the first place. All I've ended up doing is making life more difficult for both of us.'

'Are you sure about that? Oh, maybe it feels like that at

the moment but sometimes you need to work through the problems before you can understand what's really going on.' She shrugged. 'I get the impression that you and Morgan never really dealt with your problems in the past.'

'I tried, believe me, but it wasn't easy. We found out that we couldn't have children, you see. It was a huge blow for both of us, and especially for Morgan when he discovered that he could never father a child. I tried to make him understand that it made no difference to how I felt about him, but he decided that it wouldn't be fair to me if we stayed together. I couldn't seem to make him see sense.'

'No wonder. You were probably too upset yourself at the time. I know I would have been.' Maggie squeezed her hand. 'But the situation has changed because there's Tomàs to consider now. Are you sure that you can't make Morgan see that this might be the fresh start you both need?'

'You mean that we should get back together?' She heard the incredulity in her voice and frowned when Maggie laughed.

'Yes. Come on, Katrina, surely the idea must have occurred to you? Why did you decide to ask Morgan for help with the adoption if you didn't want to give your marriage a second chance?'

'B-because it meant that I would have a better chance of persuading the authorities to let me adopt Tomàs if he helped me. I mean, then he'd have two parents, a mother and a father...' She trailed off uncertainly because it was impossible to ignore the way her heart seemed to be racing all of a sudden.

'And that's the only reason, is it? You'd be prepared to put your hand on your heart and swear that in a court of law?' Maggie's tone was gentle. 'I think you're fooling yourself if you believe that. It's obvious that you're still in love with Morgan. The question now is what are you going to do about it?'

Katrina's mouth felt so dry that she couldn't speak. She

could feel the heavy beat of her heart shaking her. She wasn't in love with Morgan. She couldn't be! And yet...

She closed her eyes as her mind spun with conflicting thoughts. It was hard to make sense of them all, impossible to sort out her feelings and arrange them in neat little compartments. Everything was all ravelled up together—what had happened in the past, what was happening now—so that it was difficult to think clearly. Then slowly one thought began to surface through all the others. How would she feel if she was told that she would never see Morgan again?

She opened her eyes and looked at Maggie, knowing that there was no way that she could lie to herself any longer. 'I don't know what I'm going to do but you're right. I do love him. I always have.'

'Thank heavens for that!' Maggie laughed, obviously trying to lighten the mood a little. 'I was starting to think that I might be suffering from pre-wedding delusions.'

'No, don't worry. I think you can safely claim that you're as sane as the rest of us—probably saner, in fact,' Katrina added ruefully.

'Thanks. That's just what I needed to hear.' She quickly propelled Katrina along the corridor to the physiotherapy unit then paused outside the waiting-room door. 'I hope you'll find a way to work things out, Katrina. Really I do. Love is too precious to lose.'

'I know, although I'm not sure that there's a way to resolve this situation.' She returned the other woman's hug then took a deep breath. 'Right, no more soul-searching. Onwards and upwards, as they say!'

Maggie laughed as she wheeled her inside. Katrina waved her off then waited for Danny to call her through for her appointment. The odd thing was that she felt strangely at peace at last.

She loved Morgan. Even if he no longer loved her, it

didn't change how she felt. Maggie had asked her what she was going to do about it but she wasn't sure if there was anything she *could* do. She certainly wouldn't risk causing him more heartache by telling him how she felt.

CHAPTER ELEVEN

'THIS should never have happened! It's nothing short of incompetence and the person responsible shouldn't be allowed to call himself a surgeon!'

Morgan deftly broke the bone then glanced at Cheryl across the operating table. 'This poor boy will have to put up with wearing a cast for another ten weeks.'

'It's a shame,' Cheryl agreed, glancing at the teenager.

Adam Marshall had been referred to them by his GP after complaining of continued pain in his right ankle. The boy had suffered a Pott's fracture whilst playing football six months earlier. His fibula—the outer of the two bones in his lower leg—had fractured just above the ankle and his tibia, or shinbone, had been fractured as well. Treatment had consisted of manipulating both bones back into place under general anaesthetic, followed by immobilisation of the foot, ankle and lower leg in a cast.

That should have been the end of the matter, but as soon as Morgan had examined the boy he had known that things hadn't gone according to plan. Adam's ankle had been grossly deformed because the bones had reunited at the wrong angle. Morgan had had no choice but to operate and rebreak them so that they could heal correctly. However, it annoyed him intensely that the boy could have been spared this added ordeal if the surgeon who had dealt with him previously had done a better job.

'If this is an example of the standard of work that they were happy with at the Royal then it's a good job that their orthopaedic department has been closed down.' He manoeuvred the ends of the tibia together and started to screw them into place.

'I heard that the staff got very dispirited when they heard about the closure,' Cheryl observed.

'Maybe they did but it's no excuse.' Morgan realised how that had sounded and sighed because he hadn't meant to snap at poor Cheryl. It was just unfortunate that she always seemed to be around when he was feeling particularly edgy. 'Sorry, I wasn't getting at you. It just annoys me when I see something like this.'

'That's all right,' she replied immediately. 'And I agree with you. I think it's deplorable that any surgeon should be happy with such a shoddy job!'

His brows rose because it wasn't usual for her to speak with such vehemence. 'I'm glad we're in such accord.' He came to a swift decision, prompted by a desire to encourage her new-found confidence. 'So, how about sorting out the mess that was made of the fibula?'

'Oh, are you sure?' Cheryl sounded a little breathless at the idea of being asked to take over.

He smiled reassuringly. 'I wouldn't have suggested it if I didn't think you could do the job, Dr Rothwell.'

He changed places with her, keeping well back so that she wouldn't think that he was worried she wouldn't do a good job. He was delighted by how well she had risen to the challenge and said so as they left Theatre together a short time later.

'That was excellent work, Cheryl. Well done.'

'Thank you, sir!' She was positively glowing with happiness as she went rushing off to the locker rooms to change.

Morgan smiled to himself as he stripped off his gown and tossed it into the bin. It was good to know that he had made someone happy!

The thought was like a dash of cold water because it reminded him of how unhappy Katrina had looked that morning before he'd left home. It didn't make him feel good to know that she'd been upset by the cool way he'd been treating her, but there was nothing else he could do when he was terrified of letting her see how he really felt. He loved her so much but it was his problem, not hers.

It was a sobering thought and it preyed on his mind for the rest of the day. By the time he drew up in front of the flat that night, he was dreading the coming evening. Being with Katrina was both a pleasure and a pain because he needed to watch every word he said. It made him wonder how long he could keep it up, yet what was the alternative? Telling her that he was still madly in love with her was out of the question!

Tomàs must have heard him coming in because he came hurtling down the hall. Morgan picked him up and settled him on his shoulders. There was a deliciously spicy smell wafting from the kitchen so he headed straight there, expecting to find Mrs Mackenzie cooking their evening meal. It came as a shock when he discovered Katrina, perched on a stool beside the cooker, stirring a bubbling pot of spaghetti sauce.

'What on earth are you doing?' he demanded, setting Tomàs down.

'Cooking, unless I'm very much mistaken.' She stared defiantly back at him, her hazel eyes glittering with challenge as she dared him to say anything else. 'Mrs Mackenzie had a dental appointment so I made her go home early.'

'I see. And do you think it's a good idea for you to be doing that?' he asked as calmly as he could.

He took a deep breath but the sight of her sitting there, her face flushed with heat, her hair in a glorious tangle was playing havoc with his resolve. How in heaven's name could he *distance* himself when all he wanted was to sweep her into his arms and kiss her until both of them were dizzy?

'Yes. I refuse to be treated like an invalid. I have a

broken leg, that's all. People manage to function perfectly well with a lot worse things wrong with them!'

She gave the pan another quick stir then went to get up. Morgan stepped forward and quickly caught hold of her arm as she swayed perilously. He drew her against him to steady her, trying not to notice the warmth of her body as it rested against his, but that was like asking the sun not to shine or the tide not to turn. How could he be this close to her and not notice every little thing about her? he wondered sickly.

'I'm fine now. If you could just pass me those crutches, please.'

He jumped when he realised that he still had hold of her. Looking round, he frowned when he saw the metal crutches propped against the worktop. 'Did you get those today? I didn't think you'd be ready for crutches just yet.'

'Danny said that I'm a model patient and that he wished all his patients were so good about doing their exercises,' she told him firmly. 'That's why he decided to let me have crutches, although I'm still a bit wobbly on them.'

'I can imagine. It takes a bit of time to get used to them.' He fetched the crutches, waiting until she had slid her arms into the supports before stepping back.

She took a few careful steps, much to Tomàs's delight. He danced around her as she crossed the kitchen, almost tripping her up in his eagerness to keep up with her.

'Careful! You don't want Mummy falling over and hurting her leg again,' Morgan warned, quickly steering the child out of the way.

'It's all a big game to Tomàs but I want to get as much practice as I can. It will make it easier.'

'To get around the flat, you mean?' he queried, wondering what had caused the sudden edge in her voice.

'Easier when I go home to Derby.' She took a deep breath. 'I appreciate you offering to let me stay here, Morgan, but I think it would be best if I went home as soon as possible. I'll get in touch with the social services department and ask if they can arrange for me to have a home help. Most local authorities make provision for a situation like this.'

He didn't know what to say. Part of him wanted to argue that the idea was ridiculous, that even with help she would find it extremely hard to manage. However, he couldn't ignore the fact that having her stay at the flat would grow increasingly difficult.

Could he honestly bear to be around her, day after day, and not tell her that he loved her? Yet how could he tell her that when it was probably the last thing that she would want to hear? The thought was so bitterly painful that afterwards he wasn't sure how he had managed to hide it from her. Only a deep-seated reluctance to let her see how vulnerable he was steeled his resolve. The one thing he wouldn't countenance was making her feel sorry for him!

'If that's your decision, I won't try to persuade you to change your mind.'

Morgan shrugged, wondering how it was possible to act as though it didn't matter when it felt as though his heart was breaking. Once Katrina went home, he would never see her again. She had only come to find him because of Tomàs, and now that he wouldn't help her he was of no more use to her. It seemed rather apt in a way. What use was a man like him to a woman who wanted children?

'When are you planning on leaving?' he asked, hoping that she couldn't hear the raw note of agony in his voice. He had tried to disguise it but he wasn't sure that he'd succeeded when he saw her gaze sharpen.

'The end of the week. I should be a bit more proficient on these by then.' Katrina glanced at the crutches then looked at him, and he felt his stomach clench when he saw the expression in her eyes, a mixture of hope and longing that he couldn't understand.

'You're sure you don't mind, Morgan? I don't want you to think that I'm ungrateful...'

'Of course not,' he said quickly, because he simply couldn't bear to stand there and discuss her departure any longer. In another few seconds he would do the unforgivable and beg her to stay, admit that he couldn't bear the thought of living the rest of his life without her. How could he even think of stooping so low as to emotionally blackmail her into staying when it was patently obvious that it was the last thing she wanted to do?

'Good. That's all right, then.'

She gave him a bright smile and went back to the stove. Morgan watched while she got herself comfortable on the stool once more but there didn't seem to be anything else to say.

He left the kitchen and went to get changed, with Tomàs skipping along beside him, chattering nineteen to the dozen. He tried his best to respond but it was impossible when it felt as though something inside him had died. In a few more days Katrina would be gone for ever. How could he bear it?

Katrina turned on the television, needing something to fill the silence and stop her thinking about what she had done. Funnily enough, she hadn't planned on telling Morgan that she was leaving, but she knew that she had done the right thing. He certainly hadn't tried to persuade her to reconsider!

She clamped down on that painful thought as he came back after putting Tomàs to bed. If she was to get through the next few days relatively unscathed, she couldn't afford to think like that.

'Is he asleep?' she asked, forcing herself to smile as he sat down in the chair.

'Flat out. What are you watching?'

'Oh, nothing really. You choose.' She passed him the

remote-control, feeling her heart somersault when his fingers brushed hers. A flurry raced through her nerve endings and she bit her lip. Just a touch was all it took, the merest brushing of skin against skin, and her blood was racing, her heart pounding. How could she bear to leave him when she loved him so much? How could she bear to stay when he would never love her?

It was simply too much to hope that she could sit there and pretend that everything was all right when it felt as though her world was falling apart. She rose clumsily to her feet, ignoring the hand he offered her. She couldn't bear to have him touch her right then, to feel his hand, warm and strong, on hers, otherwise she would break down.

'I think I'll wash my hair. Mrs Mackenzie helped me take a shower this morning but I didn't like to be any more of a nuisance.'

'Are you sure you can manage?' he said immediately, half rising.

'Yes!' She quickly moderated her tone when she saw him frown. 'Sorry. I didn't mean to snap. I just find it difficult not being able to do things for myself.'

'I understand, but promise that you'll call me if you get stuck.'

'I shall.'

Katrina took her time as she crossed the room, aware of how easy it would be to slip on the polished floor. Although the crutches had rubber tips, she still wasn't that confident using them. She breathed a sigh of relief when she made it safely to the bathroom because it was another hurdle that she had overcome. By the end of the week she should be a lot more used to getting around unaided and should be able to do more for herself when she returned home. She had to concentrate on getting her life back together and put this unhappy episode behind her.

She managed to wash her hair but drying it proved a herculean task. The drier was a very high-tech, wall-

mounted one, and the cord simply wouldn't stretch enough
so that she could sit down while she used it. Her leg had
started to throb painfully, probably because she had tried
doing too much, and she desperately needed to rest it. In
the end she simply gave up. She would just have to put up
with wet hair!

Morgan frowned when she went back into the sitting
room. 'Aren't you going to dry your hair?'

'I couldn't manage it with the drier in the bathroom,' she
explained shortly, stifling a groan as she sank onto the sofa.

'Is your leg hurting?' he guessed astutely, watching her
grimace.

'Just a bit. And before you say anything, yes, I probably
have done too much.'

He sighed deeply although his eyes were concerned. 'I
did warn you, Katrina. There's no point trying to run before
you can walk.'

'There's not much danger of that!' she snapped, then
suddenly realised that he was smiling. She found herself
smiling as well when she thought about what he had said.
'Oh, ha, ha, very funny!'

'I try my best,' he replied drolly, getting up. 'Anyway,
stay there and I'll fetch the drier from my room. We can't
have you catching a chill to add to your woes.'

He came back a few minutes later with a hairdrier and
plugged it in. He had also thought to bring a brush with
him and he put it down on the back of the sofa.

'Your hair is in a real tangle. Lean forward while I brush
it for you.' Before she could object, he picked up a long
strand of her hair and started working the knots out of it.

'You don't need to do that,' she said quickly, trying to
wriggle out of his reach.

'I know I don't. But it will be easier if I brush out all
the tangles before you dry it.'

Katrina wasn't sure what to do. She didn't want to make
a fuss but the feel of his hands as he worked the brush

through her hair was having the strangest effect. She closed her eyes when she felt a sensual ripple dance across her scalp as he picked up another strand and began easing the knots out of it.

'I'm not hurting you, am I?' he said softly, his hands stilling for a moment.

'No, it's fine,' she whispered, feeling a wave of heat flowing through her when she heard the husky note in her voice.

She kept her eyes tightly shut while she willed herself to remain calm, but it was impossible when her blood seemed to be heating by the second. Each time Morgan drew the bristles of the brush across her scalp another river of sensation flowed through her, adding to the overall feeling of heat and excitement that was building inside her. When he put down the brush and picked up the drier she knew that she should tell him that she could manage from there on, but she simply didn't have the will-power to stop what was happening, to deny herself the sheer delight of feeling his hands touching her, caressing her, loving her...

Her eyes flew open and she gasped because the idea was so absurd that she could barely believe that she had thought it. Morgan switched off the drier and the ensuing silence seemed deafening. She could feel her pulse beating away at her throat and wrists, feel it beating in other more intimate places, a hot pulsing that seemed to run deeper and deeper until her very soul seemed to vibrate with its force.

'Katrina.'

Her name was as gentle as a breeze on a summer's day, as soft as a snowflake falling. She heard it with her ears and felt it with every shred of her being. Morgan said her name as though it were the most beautiful sound in the world, lovelier than the loveliest music, sweeter than the sweetest tune. He said it with warmth, with passion, with so many other emotions that it made her feel dizzy because she couldn't sort out one from another, until it dawned on her that there was no need to worry about that. Why try examining what he had meant when it was so much easier simply to feel?

His skin felt feverishly hot as he bent and brushed his cheek against hers. He was still standing behind the sofa and she felt him tug gently on her hair to bring her head back so that he could reach her mouth. She turned towards him, blindly searching for his lips, feeling her heart lift like a bird in flight when they found hers.

The kiss was everything she could have dreamed of, so tender that it brought tears to her eyes, so passionate that it made the pulsing inside her grow even more fierce. It was as though four years of longing and abstinence had been distilled into a single kiss so that she found herself wondering if she would ever experience anything more potent again in the whole of her life. And yet all it took was the gentle brush of his fingers as they slid over her shoulder and came to rest on the swell of her breast to show her that there were more delights still to come.

Katrina moaned softly when she felt his thumb rubbing her hardening nipple. Even though she was fully dressed, the sensations it aroused were exquisite. She arched her back, inciting him to touch her again, feeling her breath catch so tightly that she could barely breathe when his other hand slid down and found her other breast.

'I want to touch you properly,' he grated, his voice sounding hoarse, his breathing laboured. 'I want to feel your skin properly, touch it, caress, bury myself in your softness.'

She reached up behind her, letting her fingers slide into the dark silk of his hair as she drew his head down so that she could kiss him. 'I want that, too, Morgan,' she whispered against his mouth. 'I want it so much...'

She didn't finish the sentence—couldn't, because he was kissing her again with a passion that stole her ability to think, let alone speak. When he came around the sofa and swept her up in his arms she clung to him, her arms twining around his neck, holding him as closely and as tightly as he held her.

He carried her into his bedroom and laid her on the bed then sat down beside her and switched on the bedside lamp, tilting the shade so that it didn't glare into her eyes. Katrina bit her lip because the expression on his face as he gently drew the sweatshirt over her head made her want to cry. She couldn't recall ever seeing such yearning on anyone's face before. But, then, she couldn't see the expression on her own face—maybe it was just the same?

He slid the tips of his fingers beneath the strap of her bra and eased it off her shoulder until the lace cup fell away from her breast. Bending, he placed his mouth to her nipple, letting his tongue circle the swollen tip time after time until she was almost mindless with the sensations that were rippling through her.

He drew back, smiling gently when she immediately reached for him. 'I'm not going anywhere. Just let me get rid of some of this clothing. OK?'

He stood up and stripped off his shirt, dragging it over his head and tossing it onto the floor with a careless disregard. Katrina felt the pulsing inside her grow even stronger as she looked at him standing there, his powerful chest bare except for the dark hair that curled crisply across it. When he sat down beside her again, she placed her palm flat against his chest, loving the feel of that hair curling around her fingers, enjoying the sense of power it gave her when she felt him shudder.

He eased her back against the pillows and kissed her again, slowly, letting his tongue slide inside her mouth and tangle with hers in a rhythm that stirred her unbearably. Katrina shifted restlessly as she felt the heat building inside her, felt the throbbing beat of desire growing stronger. When he stood and gently drew her skirt down over her hips, taking the utmost care not to jolt her injured leg, she was trembling with need.

He tossed her skirt onto the floor then shed his trousers before lying beside her again. All she had on were her bra and a pair of cotton briefs, and they were soon dispensed with in the same exquisitely gentle manner so that a moment later she was lying naked before him in the lamplight.

'You're so beautiful,' he whispered, bending so that he could press his mouth to the hollow of her shoulder before letting it move to the soft curve of her breast.

Katrina shivered delicately as ripple after ripple of sensation poured along her veins as his mouth followed the gentle curves of her body, stopping frequently to taste and enjoy her soft flesh. It was as though he were mapping the very contours of her body, storing up the details, wanting there to be no mistake in his mind as to her shape and form. It was the most exquisitely sensual experience that she'd ever enjoyed and her murmurs of encouragement made that plain.

His lips skimmed down her uninjured thigh to the bend of her knee while he pressed kisses against it, then moved to her calf. She moaned softly, wondering why nobody had ever told her just how potent it was to be kissed there. She was finding it increasingly difficult to hold onto her control as the passion built inside her, great waves of longing and desire that swept so languorously and seductively through her body.

When Morgan's mouth touched her instep and she felt the tip of his tongue teasing her skin she cried out, tipped over the edge by the sheer force of her need for him. She was already reaching for him when he moved up to lie beside her. The weighty cast meant that her movements were restricted but Morgan carefully positioned her so that it wouldn't be a hindrance.

He rose up above her and she could feel the heavy pulsing of his body against her as he looked deep into her eyes.

'No woman will ever be loved as I shall love you tonight, Katrina,' he murmured hoarsely.

She felt her eyes fill with tears, felt her heart fill with pain, felt her soul cry out in anguish. She didn't want him to love her just for that one night! She wanted him to love her for ever, but maybe that was wishing for the impossible. Maybe it was better to have something rather than nothing, to share this one night of passion with him to see her through all the lonely nights to come.

'Just love me, Morgan,' she said simply, drawing him to her. 'For however long and in whichever way you can…'

CHAPTER TWELVE

DAWN came in a rush, the first pale rays of light racing across the sky as though the day was in a hurry to begin.

Morgan lay on his side and watched the night fading away with a heavy heart. It had been the most wonderful night of his life and he couldn't bear to think that it was over, but now he had to decide what he would do. Should he tell Katrina that he loved her? The situation hadn't changed. He still couldn't give her the children she had always yearned for so would it be right?

'Are you awake?'

He tensed when he realised that she was awake because he'd hoped to have a few more minutes to make up his mind. He turned to face her, feeling his heart surge when he saw how beautiful she looked, lying beside him with her face softly flushed with sleep.

It was an image that he had conjured up more times than he could count in the past few years, but did he have the right to try and keep her with him so that he could wake every morning with her lying beside him? It was the fear that he might be doing the wrong thing that was so hard to deal with.

'What is it?' She touched his cheek and he shivered when he felt how cold her fingers were. 'I can tell that something is worrying you, Morgan, so, please, tell me what's wrong.'

He sighed deeply, wondering how to reply, wondering if there were words to explain how confused he felt. 'I was just thinking about what happened.'

'You mean us making love?' she said sharply, in a tone that made him flinch.

'Yes.' He caught hold of her hand and moved it away from his face, needing to get his thoughts into order—an impossibility if she continued touching him like that. Even now he could feel the first stirrings of desire building, feel his blood heating all over again. It would be so easy to let passion sweep them away again but it would be the wrong thing to do when they needed to talk about what had happened and what it had meant—to both of them.

A feeling of intense coldness flowed through him all of a sudden as he considered that thought. Last night he had been swept away by his desire for Katrina and knew that she had been swept away by desire, too. But had it really *meant* anything to her? Or had it simply been an outpouring of sexual desire?

He wasn't naïve enough to believe that women weren't capable of sexual feelings just as men were. So had that been the reason why she had given herself to him last night with such abandon? He had no idea if she'd had a relationship whilst she'd been working overseas, but she had always enjoyed their love-making in the past. Maybe her passion last night had been the result of abstinence and he'd just happened to be there, ready and more than willing to satisfy her needs.

'For heaven's sake, Morgan, say something!' She gave a harsh little laugh that brought his eyes flying to her face, and he frowned when he saw the angry colour in her cheeks. 'I promise you that I won't go to pieces if you tell me the truth!'

'And what truth might that be?' he asked, unable to keep the bite out of his voice because such thoughts were playing havoc with him. 'That last night was a highly enjoyable experience but that was all it was? That it didn't mean that we were promising one another undying love and devotion?'

He took a deep breath in an effort to control the pain

that was twisting his heart. 'That it wasn't the prelude to our reconciliation?'

'Yes! That sounds about right to me.' She gave him a brilliant smile. 'At least we both know where we stand now. It's so much better to tell the truth, I always find, rather than run the risk of any future misunderstandings.'

'Oh, I'm sure there isn't much chance of that happening, Katrina.'

He tossed back the quilt, unable to lie there while his dreams were shattered into hundreds of tiny, irreparable pieces. Maybe he had only dreamt them for one night because he certainly hadn't allowed himself such a luxury before, but it still hurt unbearably.

He picked up his robe and dragged it on, tightening the belt with hands that shook. Katrina was still lying in the bed and he made himself look at her because it wasn't fair to make her feel that she had done something wrong when all she'd done had been to tell him the truth.

'I'll go and wake Tomàs. Stay there for a moment. I'll fetch you a robe once he's having his breakfast.'

'Thank you.'

Her voice was little above a whisper and Morgan frowned when he heard the quavery note it held. Just for a second he wondered if he had made a mistake about last night and what it had meant to her, but if he had, why hadn't she said so? Why had she agreed with him when she could have told him that his assumptions had been horribly wrong?

He swung round, realising how pointless it was to stand there thinking about it. Katrina had told him the truth and he should respect her for not having lied. She could very easily have done so because he'd been more than ready to believe her if she'd said that she still loved him.

If she'd told him that, he would have done anything in the world to make sure that they were never parted again. He would even have agreed to help her adopt Tomàs so that they could have the family they had yearned for. How sad that now he would have welcomed the idea when four years ago he had refused to consider it. If anyone was to blame for the mess he'd made of his life, it was himself!

Katrina lay in bed after Morgan had left the room, wondering if it was actually possible for a heart to break. It felt as though hers had done so when he'd admitted that last night had meant nothing to him. Maybe she could have fooled herself into thinking that he'd lied, but he'd been far too blunt for that.

Last night had been an enjoyable experience, and that was all!

She quickly wiped all expression from her face as he came back with her robe. He laid it on the bed where she could reach it then looked at her. She steeled herself when she felt his searching green gaze travelling over her face because she refused to make a fool of herself by letting him see how hurt she was. Morgan had told her the truth and she should be grateful for that.

'Tomàs is having his breakfast so the coast is clear if you want to get up. I told him that you were in the bathroom.'

'Thank you.' She took a deep breath then reached for the robe. 'It's best not to confuse him. He'll find it difficult enough when we leave here because he's grown fond of you.'

'I've grown very fond of him, too,' he said quietly. 'Maybe you could write to me occasionally and let me know how he is getting on?'

'I really don't think there would be any point in that. I doubt if we'll see you again once we leave here.'

She slid her arms into the robe then tossed back the quilt. She frowned when she glanced up and saw the anguish on his face. It was on the tip of her tongue to ask him what was wrong before she thought better of it. Maybe she'd had enough truth for one day.

Morgan helped her to the bathroom then went away to find her crutches. She thanked him politely when he brought them back then closed the door. Hobbling to the basin, she turned on the taps and stood there, letting the water flow away while she stared at herself in the mirror.

There was a new sadness in her eyes that hadn't been there before. When she and Morgan had split up four years ago it had broken her heart, but not completely. There had been one tiny corner which had remained intact, the corner where hope had clung and been nurtured during those years apart. Now that hope had died a painful death. When she left him this time it really would be the end.

'I shall be really sorry to lose you, Katrina.'

Katrina summoned a smile as Danny passed her the weights. They were nearing the end of a particularly gruelling physio session, the very last one she would have with Danny, in fact. It was Friday afternoon and tomorrow morning a car would arrive to take her back to Derby.

Morgan had made all the arrangements with his customary attention to detail, liaising with the social services department in Derby for a home help to visit her daily until her leg had healed and ordering and paying for a supply of groceries from the local supermarket to be delivered to her each week.

He had brushed aside her protests in his usual high-handed manner by telling her that it was all arranged so there was no point arguing. She knew that he had done everything he could to make her return home as easy as possible, but he hadn't been able to do the one thing she longed for most. He hadn't been able to give her his love, and her life would be empty for ever more without it.

'I bet you say that to all your patients,' she said lightly, trying not to dwell on that painful thought.

'Only the ones who work hard,' he assured her, grinning. 'Most folk seem to think that they'll get better by magic. They don't seem to realise that they need to put some effort into it.'

'If that's a hint then I'm trying, I'm trying!' She lifted the weights then slowly lowered them to her sides. 'I'll have muscles to die for soon!'

'Don't knock it!' Danny laughed. 'A lot of women would love to be as fit as you are, with or without that cast. Talking of which, I've just taken on Sandra Sullivan as my latest patient. She's certainly had the stuffing knocked out of her.'

'Have the police found her husband?' she asked curiously.

'Yes. Found him, charged him and let him out on bail.' Danny shrugged. 'Evidently, he isn't considered a threat to society so the magistrates decided to let him go.'

'Really?' She was appalled. 'He should have been locked up and the key thrown away, to my mind. What if he tries to see Sandra?'

'Oh, the staff on the surgical ward have been warned not to admit him,' he assured her. 'Sandra's pretty safe while she's in here. Actually, you might see her on your way out because she's my next patient.'

He checked his work sheet and grinned. 'Then I've got this young lad called Adam Marshall. He pleaded to have extra physio so I'm seeing him daily. The kid's mad about football so it's a case of hero-worship, I'm afraid.'

He held up his hands and wiggled his fingers. 'These hands have touched the feet of his favourite team!'

Katrina laughed. 'I never realised how honoured I was.'

'Count yourself lucky, young lady. Not everyone gets my personal attention. If it hadn't been for your husband, I doubt whether you would have been one of the chosen few!'

She managed to smile because she didn't want Danny to

suspect that anything was wrong. Her husband, but for how long? What point was there in them remaining married now?

It was a sobering thought and it kept her company while she completed her exercises. She thanked Danny for everything he had done then went back to the waiting room. A porter would collect her shortly and take her back to Reception to wait for the ambulance. There were two more patients already there and she smiled when she realised that Sandra was one of them.

'How are you?' she asked, going over to sit beside her wheelchair. Danny had gone back into the treatment room to sort out the equipment he would be using, so she knew that they would have a few minutes to chat.

'A lot better than I was.' Sandra sighed as she glanced at the casts on her arms. 'It's going to take a while before I can get rid of these, though.'

'I just wish that you'd told us what had been happening,' Katrina said sympathetically. 'Maybe we could have done something to help you.'

'I was too scared. It's hard to imagine what it's like, living in fear every day of your life,' Sandra explained. 'It saps your will after a time. I don't really know how I plucked up the courage to try and leave Antony in the first place. I certainly wouldn't have attempted it if he hadn't been sent away on business. But then I had to go and make a mess of things by crashing the car. I knew he would be furious when he found out, because he'd told me what he would do if I ever tried to leave him. When he came into the ward that night I just panicked and made a run for it.'

'I understand, really I do. It must have been a nightmare. But where did you go when you left the hospital, and how did he find you?'

'I stayed in a B and B not far from here. I didn't care where I went so long as he couldn't track me down, but I needed a place to rest until I felt well enough to move to a different part of the country.'

Sandra sighed. 'I had to go home and get some clothes to take with me so I chose a time when I was sure that Antony would be at work. However, it turned out that he had taken time off sick. He must have known that I would go home at some point, and he was waiting for me.'

'How awful! It doesn't bear thinking about—' Katrina began, then looked up when the door burst open. She felt herself go cold when she recognised the man who had come into the room as Sandra's husband. But it wasn't just the sight of him which terrified her, it was what he was holding. Her heart began to pound when she saw the shotgun in his hands.

Sandra let out a shrill scream of terror which brought Danny racing from his office. Katrina saw him stop when Sullivan levelled the gun at him.

'Stay out of this. It's got nothing to do with you.' He glanced at Sandra and smiled grimly. 'This is between me and my wife.'

'Look, let's try to be sensible…' Danny began but didn't get any further as the waiting-room door opened once more.

Katrina wasn't sure what happened next because everything moved so fast. One minute the porter who had come to collect her was standing in the doorway and the next minute there was a loud explosion.

She instinctively ducked as bits of plaster rained down from the ceiling then cried out in horror as Danny leapt forward to tackle Sullivan and was struck a glancing blow across his right temple with the butt of the gun. He fell to the floor, unconscious.

Sandra was rocking to and fro in her distress. 'He's going to kill us, he's going to kill us all,' she kept repeating in a keening wail.

Katrina put her hand on Sandra's shoulder. 'It will be all right. Everything will be all right. Shh, now.'

'Everyone get inside. Now!'

Sullivan pointed to the treatment room with the barrel of
the gun. There was a gash on his forehead from when he'd
been struck by some falling plaster and a wildness in his
eyes that warned her he was within a hairsbreadth of losing
control, so she got up as quickly as she could and asked
young Adam Marshall, the other patient, to help her push
Sandra into the room.

Sullivan slammed the door as soon as they were inside
then ordered them to sit down. Katrina tried to calm a sobbing Sandra as she slowly sat down in a chair beside her.
She had no idea what was going to happen but suddenly
the thought that she could die in this room without having
told Morgan that she loved him was the most terrifying
thought of all. She made herself a solemn promise that if
she did get through this, she would tell him the truth.

Morgan was on his way out of Theatre when news of what
had happened reached him. He was just wondering if there
was anything he could do to help when Luke came to find
him. As soon as he saw the expression on the younger
man's face, he felt his stomach sink.

'Katrina's one of the patients who was in Physio when
Sullivan broke in,' Luke told him. 'Apparently, she was
waiting for the porter to collect her.'

'Hell!'

The single word was all he could manage as fear twisted
his insides into knots. Tossing his gown into the basket, he
ran out of the anteroom, uncaring that he almost knocked
over Dave Carson in his haste. The police had cordoned
off the area around the physiotherapy unit so he went
straight to the officer in charge.

'My wife is one of the patients Sullivan is holding hos-
tage,' he explained tersely. 'My name is Morgan Grey and
I'm head of orthopaedic surgery here.'

'Come with me, sir.' The constable took him straight to his senior officer and introduced him.

'What's happening now?' Morgan demanded.

'At the moment we are trying to keep things as calm as possible, Dr Grey. The last thing we want to do is to panic Sullivan.'

'So that means we just sit around doing nothing until he makes up his mind what he wants?' he snapped.

'Basically, yes.'

The officer moved away as one of his men called him over. Morgan wished he could hear what they were saying as they conferred together. He felt as though he would explode if something wasn't done soon. The thought that Katrina was in danger was more than he could bear.

How would he feel if something happened to her? he wondered sickly. How could he go on living in a world where she no longer existed? It didn't bear thinking about, but it made him see what a fool he had been to lie to her the other day. He should have told her that he loved her and to hell with the consequences!

'It appears that Sullivan was injured by some plaster falling from the ceiling. He wants someone to go in there and treat him,' the policeman informed him, coming back.

'I'll do it,' Morgan replied immediately. He followed the officer along the corridor, pausing briefly on the way to collect a case of basic medical supplies. There was a crowd of staff gathered around and a number of them wished him luck.

'No heroics, Dr Grey,' the other man warned as they stopped outside the waiting room. 'This is a highly volatile situation.'

'I realise that and I assure you that I have no intention of endangering any of the people in that room.'

He took a deep breath then opened the door and immediately spotted Danny lying on the floor. He ran straight over to him, but before he could check how badly injured he was the door to the treatment room opened and Katrina appeared on her crutches. He saw the relief that crossed her face when she recognised him.

'Morgan! What are you doing here?' she began, before she was roughly pushed aside as Sullivan appeared.

Morgan managed to hang onto his temper with considerable effort as the man indicated that he should enter the room. How dare he treat Katrina that way?

It was an effort to contain his anger as he dealt with the gash on Sullivan's temple. It wasn't deep, although it had obviously bled heavily, so he used a row of butterfly stitches to close it. No one had said a word while he'd been attending to the man, although he'd been aware of Katrina's eyes watching him the whole time.

He glanced at her, willing her to understand that he wouldn't let anything bad happen to her while there was breath left in his body. He would give up his own life willingly and without hesitation if it meant that he could save her.

She gave him a gentle smile in return and he felt his heart lift because there was something in her eyes at that moment which he had never thought he would see again...

'Tell the police that I want a guarantee that I won't be stopped when I leave here.'

Morgan forced himself to concentrate. 'Why don't you end this right now? You know very well that you won't get away with it.'

'Do I? Well, Doctor, I beg to differ. I have two women and a boy here who will be my passport out of here. The police won't want to run the risk of anything happening to them.'

'So they are your passport to freedom?' He smiled sardonically. 'How far do you think you'll get with them in tow? The boy can barely walk, your wife's in a wheelchair and Katrina is on crutches.'

'Katrina? So you know her, do you?' Sullivan smiled, a

taunting light appearing in his eyes as he looked at Katrina.
'You two are friends, then?'

'We're married,' she said sharply yet in a tone that sent
a ripple down Morgan's spine because there had been so
much *meaning* in it. It was an effort to concentrate again
when he heard Sullivan laugh.

'Are you indeed? Then I hope that your marriage is more
successful than mine has been. Still, there's always a way
out, isn't there? One guaranteed way to put an end to it
all.'

Morgan reacted instinctively when he saw Sullivan raise
the gun and aim it at Sandra. He hurled himself forward,
knocking the other man off the bench. There was a deafening explosion as he and Sullivan hit the floor with such
force that it knocked all the breath from his body.

The next few seconds were a blur. Sandra was screaming
hysterically and young Adam was shouting for the police
to come quickly. It was a relief when two police officers
helped him up then quickly handcuffed the other man and
led him away.

'Are you all right? You're not hurt? Morgan!' Suddenly
Katrina was beside him, her face paper-white with shock
as she stared at him as though she could scarcely believe
that he was all in one piece.

'I'm fine.' He summoned a smile but it was an effort and
not just because of what had happened either. All of a sudden his heart seemed to be racing twice as fast as normal,
yet the message it was sending out was one that he was
afraid to believe. Katrina *didn't* love him. She had already
told him that. So why was she looking at him like that?

In the end it was simply too much effort to work it out.
He just opened his arms and she stepped into them, mur-
muring incoherently as he folded her against him and held
her as though he would never let her go again.

'I was so scared… I thought you'd been hurt…killed…

I couldn't bear it if anything happened to you, Morgan, I couldn't bear it!'

She reached up, pressing kisses along his jaw before burrowing against him as though she needed tangible proof that he really was unharmed. Morgan bent and looked deep into her eyes so that there could be no mistake this time about what he was saying. He couldn't afford any more mistakes, not in this lifetime!

'I know how you feel, sweetheart. I felt the same when I found out that you were here. It's all part of loving someone as much as I love you. It means that you worry about them.'

'You love me?' she said, staring at him in bewilderment.

'Uh-huh.' He kissed the tip of her nose then glanced round as several members of staff suddenly appeared to tend to Danny and take Sandra and young Adam back to the ward. 'I think we should continue this conversation somewhere more private, don't you? Let's go to my office.'

'All right, but before we go I need to tell you something.'

His heart seemed to come to a standstill, no mean feat after the way it had been pumping away, because he had heard the gravity in her voice. 'And that is?' he said thickly.

'That I love you. That I never stopped loving you the whole time we were apart. That I shall never stop in all the years that are to come.' She smiled up at him, her hazel eyes ablaze with love. 'Whichever way you look at it, Morgan, I'm mad about you and always will be!'

'And I'm mad about you, my darling. For ever...' He kissed her gently then smiled at her. 'And always.'

It took them ages to reach his office because of the number of times they were stopped along the way. Everyone wanted to hear about what had happened and offer their congratulations. Katrina was positively seething with impatience by the time they got there. Morgan closed the door then drew her into his arms with undisguised relief.

'Thank heavens for that! I thought we were never going

to make it.' He kissed her quickly, his mouth telling its own tale of how much he had been longing to do so.

She kissed him back, letting all the love she had kept stored up pour out. 'I love you so much,' she whispered when they drew apart. 'I just never thought that I'd be able to tell you how much.'

'We're such idiots, aren't we?' he said tenderly, framing her face between his hands. 'We were both so determined not to hurt the other that we refused to admit how we felt.'

'Is that why you let me believe that you didn't love me?' she asked huskily.

'Yes.' She felt him take a deep breath and the emotion in his voice brought tears to her eyes. 'I didn't think it would be right to tell you how I felt when nothing had changed. I...I shall never be able to give you the children you long for, Katrina.'

'Don't!' She drew his head down, pressing her mouth to his in an attempt to ease his pain. It almost broke her heart to see him torturing himself this way when there was no need.

She brushed her lips over the dampness on his cheeks then smiled at him. 'So long as I have you, Morgan, I'll be happy. Yes, it would have been wonderful if we could have had children of our own, but if it isn't to be then I accept that. What I can't accept is living my life without you.' Her voice broke because the thought was unbearable. 'I couldn't stand that, my darling.'

'Oh, my love!' He kissed her tenderly, not attempting to hold anything back.

She smiled when they finally drew apart. 'At least we've got that straight now. Thank heavens!'

'Thank heavens, indeed!' He laughed deeply as he slid his hand under her elbow and helped her across the room. Sitting down on one of the armchairs, he pulled her onto his knee.

He treated her to another delicious kiss then looked tenderly at her. 'We may have established without the shadow of a doubt that we are both mad about one another but there are still things that we need to discuss.'

'You mean Tomàs?' She tried to keep the anxiety out of her voice but knew that she'd failed when she heard him sigh.

'Yes, but I don't want you worrying that there's a problem. I know that I said I could never help you with his adoption, but circumstances have changed.' He lifted her hand to his lips and kissed her palm. 'I hope that you'll let me be a proper father to him, Katrina, because it's what I want more than anything.'

'Are you sure? You're not just saying that because—'

'No, I'm not.' He kissed her hard, not letting her finish. 'I'm not just saying that because it's what you want me to say.' He suddenly stopped and frowned and she could see the dawning wonderment in his eyes.

'I want to help you to adopt him because it's what *I* want, because it's the right thing to do. I told you that I had grown very fond of him but it's more than that.' He squeezed her hand and she heard the catch in his voice. 'I love that child and I couldn't bear to think that I would never see him again.'

'Oh, Morgan, it's like a dream come true to hear you say that!' She kissed him quickly then drew back and frowned. 'But why were you so opposed to the idea of adoption in the first place?'

A shadow crossed his face but he met her eyes squarely. 'Because of my own experiences, of course. I think you guessed that, didn't you? That's why you asked me about my stepfather that time.'

'You don't have to tell me if you don't want to...' she began, but he shook his head.

'But I do want to. I want to get it all out into the open once and for all then put it behind me.'

Morgan took a deep breath then carried on. 'You know

that my mother remarried when I was ten, but what you don't know is how much unhappiness it caused me. My stepfather never made any bones about the fact that he wasn't interested in me. I had just come as part of the package. He'd wanted to marry my mother and had got me as an unwelcome bonus.'

'Oh, how sad!' Katrina exclaimed.

'It was, because until Mother remarried I'd been perfectly happy.' He shrugged. 'Anyway, I was sent off to boarding school not long after they married, which was a relief for all of us in a way. Things might have worked out, if not happily, at least with a degree of civility if Mother hadn't got pregnant. She and my stepfather were over the moon when my brother was born.'

'How did you feel about it?' she asked curiously, wondering how he had dealt with the new arrival.

'Funnily enough, I was thrilled. I loved Michael from the first moment I laid eyes on him and he felt the same way about me.' He smiled reflectively. 'He used to follow me everywhere whenever I came home from school and, despite the age gap, we spent hours playing together.'

'Surely that should have helped ease the situation?' she queried. 'I mean, it must have been a relief for your mother when the two of you got on so well.'

'Maybe it would have helped, but unfortunately Michael died when he was five. He'd had a heart defect that hadn't been detected when he was born, and he just died.'

He cleared his throat but she had heard the anguish in his voice and knew that he still grieved for the loss of his brother. She pressed a gentle kiss to his cheek and heard him sigh before he continued.

'Mother was devastated, of course. When I came home for Michael's funeral she could barely speak to me because she was so distraught.'

'What about your stepfather?' Katrina prompted when he paused, thinking how hard it must have been for him to deal with his own grief when there had been no one to offer any comfort.

'He was devastated as well, naturally. He didn't speak a word to me for the whole three days I was at home, in fact. Then on the day I was due to return to school he told me that he wished it had been me who had died, not Michael, that it wasn't fair that he had the responsibility of looking after another man's son when his own son was dead.'

'No! Oh, how cruel. I can't believe that anyone would say such a wicked thing to a fifteen year-old boy,' she said, appalled.

He shrugged. 'I suppose he was distraught by what had happened but I was devastated, as you can imagine. I remember protesting at the time, telling him that he was upset and that he didn't really mean it, but he just laughed. He said that the only reason he'd agreed to adopt me when he'd married my mother had been because she'd wanted him to. However, there was no chance that he would ever think of me as his own child because I could never be that. I wasn't his flesh and blood, and he would never love me.'

'And you never forgot that,' she guessed. 'You took it to heart and that's why you were so against the idea of adopting a child.'

'Yes. I was afraid that my stepfather had been right and that it wouldn't be possible to love a child that wasn't my own. The thought that I might end up hurting a child the way I had been hurt was more than I could bear,' he admitted gruffly.

'It probably also explains why you took such care to distance yourself from other people,' she suggested gently. 'It was a way to avoid being hurt the way you'd been hurt as a child.'

'That, too, although it took me a long time to admit it.' He kissed her softly and with infinite tenderness. 'It was only when you came back into my life that I started to face up to the truth, in fact, and try to deal with it.'

'And do you think you have dealt with it?' She took a quick breath but this was too important to make any mistakes about. 'You just said that you wanted to help me adopt Tomàs, but are you sure it's what you really want, Morgan?'

'Yes,' he said simply, and there was no way that she could doubt that he was telling her the truth.

Tears streamed down her face as she buried her head in his shoulder and wept. It was as though all the pain and heartache, the fear and uncertainty had suddenly found an outlet. The most touching thing of all was to discover that Morgan was crying as well.

'We're a right pair,' he declared, smiling at her.

'We are,' she agreed, hunting a tissue out of her pocket and drying her eyes. 'But that's what makes us special. We're a pair, a couple, two people who can't live without each other.'

'No, that's not quite right.' His smile was tender. 'There aren't just two of us now but three. You, me and—'

'Tomàs,' she said quickly, feeling joy fill her heart.

He kissed her quickly then drew back, and she knew that she had never seen such happiness on anyone's face before.

'And Tomàs. Our son.'

Six months later…

'Are you ready yet? The car should be here in five minutes' time…'

Morgan's voice tailed off as he opened the bedroom door and caught sight of Katrina.

'Will I do?' she asked, standing up and smiling at him.

'You most certainly will. You look beautiful,' he said huskily, walking further into the room and staring at her in wonderment.

She looked an absolute vision in the delicate sea-green dress which she had chosen to wear for the ceremony. It fitted her slender figure to perfection, just hinting at the curves beneath in a way that immediately made his blood heat. She had decided to wear fresh flowers in her hair and he sniffed appreciatively as she came towards him.

'You smell beautiful, too,' he growled, sweeping her into his arms and holding her close.

The past six months had been the most wonderful of his entire life so that each day he pinched himself when he woke to prove that he wasn't dreaming. Katrina had given up her flat in Derby and had moved into his flat, although they were now looking for somewhere more suitable to live—a house with a garden for Tomàs to play in.

They intended to stay in Dalverston because they'd both decided that it was what they wanted to do. Life was working out perfectly, in fact, and once today was over Morgan knew that the future would be all he had dreamed it could be. He couldn't believe how lucky he was and said so, earning himself a kiss.

'I feel the same,' Katrina confessed, staring up at him with a wealth of love in her eyes. 'And the wonderful thing is that life can only get better once the adoption is finalised.'

'We should get the papers through by the end of the week,' he assured her. 'So there's no need to worry that there might be a last-minute hitch.'

'I don't intend to. I mean to concentrate on what's happening today and what it means to us. It was a lovely idea to renew our wedding vows, Morgan.'

'I felt it was the right thing to do.' He kissed her tenderly. 'I want the whole world to know how much I love you, Katrina Grey.'

'Thank you.' She returned his kiss then laughed. 'And talking of the whole world, how many people did you say were coming today?'

'It's just snowballed!' He groaned. 'I've lost count of the numbers, in fact. Did I tell you that Sandra Sullivan phoned to say that she would be there?'

'I spoke to her yesterday and she said that she would try

and make it.' Katrina smiled. 'Evidently, she's bringing
Graham Walker with her. He'd seen the reports in the paper
about her husband's trial and went to see her. It seems as
though they've become quite good friends.'

'Good,' he said firmly. 'Now that Sullivan is in jail and
Sandra is divorcing him, it's about time she had some happiness in her life.'

'It is,' she agreed. 'Oh, and did you know that Maggie
and Luke are going to be there after all? Maggie rang me
last night to say that they'd managed to get a flight.'

'Wonderful!' He looked round when there was a loud
blast on a car horn outside. 'Sounds as though the car has
arrived. Are you ready, then?'

'Yes. I just need to find Tomàs…' She laughed as the
little boy came racing into the room. 'Here he is now, right
on cue.'

Morgan laughed as he bent and picked up the little boy.
He kissed the child's cheek then leant over and kissed
Katrina. There was a world of love in his eyes as he gazed
at her.

'I love you, Katrina Grey.'

'And I love you, too, Morgan,' she whispered, loving
him with her eyes.

'Then what are we waiting for?'

He caught hold of her hand and hurried her to the door,
feeling his heart swelling with joy when he heard her and
Tomàs laugh. He had a wife he adored and a son he loved.
He couldn't have asked for anything more!

Modern Romance™
...seduction and
passion guaranteed

Tender Romance™
...love affairs that
last a lifetime

Sensual Romance™
...sassy, sexy and
seductive

Blaze
...sultry days and
steamy nights

Medical Romance™
...medical drama on
the pulse

Historical Romance™
...rich, vivid and
passionate

29 new titles every month.

*With all kinds of Romance for
every kind of mood...*

MILLS & BOON®

Makes any time special™

MAT4

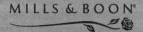

MILLS & BOON®

Medical Romance™

INNOCENT SECRET *by Josie Metcalfe*

Part 3 of Denison Memorial Hospital

Dr Joe Faraday is a man who keeps his heart hidden, and Nursing Sister Vicky Lawrence has her own secrets. She knows Joe wants her but something is holding him back. Vicky wonders if anything will tip him into her arms—and then her safety is put under threat…

HER DR WRIGHT *by Meredith Webber*

Dr Detective – Down Under

Rowena knew she was in love with her boss, Dr David Wright, and was beginning to suspect he felt the same. David was under suspicion for his wife's disappearance three years ago and Rowena desperately wanted to comfort him. But David refused to let her get involved—how could he offer her a future with his past hanging over him?

THE SURGEON'S LOVE-CHILD *by Lilian Darcy*

American surgeon Candace Fletcher feels the sizzling attraction as soon as Dr Steve Colton meets her off the plane in Australia—and the ensuing affair is passionate and intense. Then, just a few weeks before Candace is due to return home, the bombshell drops: she's pregnant!

On sale 1st March 2002

Available at most branches of WH Smith, Tesco, Martins, Borders, Eason, Sainsbury's and most good paperback bookshops. 0202/03a

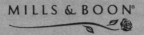

MILLS & BOON®

Medical Romance™

BACK IN HER BED *by Carol Wood*

Dr Alison Stewart ended her marriage to Sam when she accused him of having an affair, and he left for Australia. Now her determined husband is back, and the passion between them is still scorching. Sam is back in the marriage bed, but does Alison want him in her life forever?

THE FAMILY HE NEEDS *by Lucy Clark*

Reunited after ten years, it seems that surgeons Zac Carmichael and Julia Bolton are about to rekindle their relationship. But Zac's traumatic past means his instincts are to keep Julia, and her young son Edward, at a distance. Try as he might, however, he knows he can't just walk away from the family he needs...

THE CITY-GIRL DOCTOR *by Joanna Neil*

Suffering from a broken heart, Dr Jassie Radcliffe had left the city to join a challenging rural practice. Her new colleague, Dr Alex Beaufort, made it clear he didn't think she was up to the job, but secretly, he was impressed with Jassie. Then her ex-boyfriend turned up—just as Alex was falling in love with her!

On sale 1st March 2002

Available at most branches of WH Smith, Tesco, Martins, Borders, Eason, Sainsbury's and most good paperback bookshops. 0202/03b

Treat yourself this Mother's Day to the ultimate indulgence

3 brand new romance novels and a box of chocolates

= only £7.99

Available from 15th February

MIRANDA LEE

Secrets & Sins

revealed

SEDUCED BY HER BODYGUARD AND STALKED BY A STRANGER...

Available from 15th March 2002

Available at most branches of WH Smith, Tesco, Martins, Borders, Eason, Sainsbury's and most good paperback bookshops.

0402/35/MB34